OAKSEEDS
 *Stories*
from the *Land*

OAKSEEDS
Stories
from the Land

Gary W. Cook

Illustrated by Jenna Cagle

Outdoor Tennessee Series
Jim Casada, Series Editor

The University of Tennessee Press • Knoxville

To celebrate Tennessee's bicentennial in 1996, the Outdoor Tennessee Series covers a wide range of topics of interest to the general reader, including titles on the flora and fauna, the varied recreational activities, and the rich history of outdoor Tennessee. With a keen appreciation of the importance of protecting our state's natural resources and beauty, the University of Tennessee Press intends the series to emphasize environmental awareness and conservation.

Printed on
recycled paper.

The paper in this book meets the minimum requirements of the American National Standard for Permanence of Paper for Printed Library Materials. ∞ The binding materials have been chosen for strength and durability.

Library of Congress Cataloging in Publication Data

Cook, Gary W.
    Oakseeds: stories from the land / Gary W. Cook: illustrated by Jenna Cagle.—1st ed.
       p.   cm.—(Outdoor Tennessee series)
    ISBN 0-87049-801-0 (cloth: alk. paper)
    ISBN 0-87049-802-9 (pbk.: alk. paper)
    1. Outdoor life—Tennessee—Fiction. I. Title. II. Title: Oakseeds. III. Series.
    PS3553.055325O15   1993
    813' .54—dc20   92-43364
                                            CIP

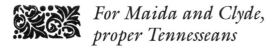 *For Maida and Clyde,*
proper Tennesseans

We must learn to reawaken and keep ourselves
awake, not by mechanical aids, but by an infinite
expectation of the dawn, which does not forsake
us in our soundest sleep.

Thoreau

 # Contents

Editor's Foreword

There is something about the South that lends itself to the making of great sporting scribes. Many of America's best-loved outdoor writers have been products of the region—North Carolina's Robert Ruark; Havilah Babcock and Archibald Rutledge from neighboring South Carolina; Mississippi's incomparable master of moonlight and magnolias, William Faulkner; and of course Tennessee's own beloved "Mr. Buck," Nash Buckingham. These writers and others of their ilk share more than roots running deeply in the southern soil. All have a profound respect, verging on reverence, for the land; all share a knack for capturing the essence of what oneness with nature can mean to the human spirit. Thanks to these gifts, such individuals have lightened the days and brightened the ways for those of us who treasure the magic and mystique of the wild world. With this book's appearance, Gary Cook bids fair to join their elevated ranks.

For many Tennesseans, Cook's literary abilities are well known. Several years ago, in a series of stories in *Tennessee Wildlife* on a wise, wonderful character, "The Old Man," he built up a devoted cadre of readers. Their ranks widened when, in 1987, Cook brought these pieces together in a book appropriately entitled *The Old Man*.

It is probably no accident, although I do not know this for a fact, that Cook's fictional figure bears more than a passing resemblance to Robert Ruark's character of the same name. After all, through the ages there has always been a special bond between the quite old and the very young as they reach across the generation separating them to form meaningful, lasting bonds. Ruark realized as much, and so does Cook.

Ruark's "Old Man" was his maternal grandfather, a sage, some-times salty individual who captured America's heart as he shaped and sustained his youthful protégé. Theirs was a timeless partnership, and the two books based on Ruark's original pieces in *Field & Stream*, *The Old Man and the Boy*, and *The Old Man's Boy Grows Older* should be required reading for every American youngster. Yet in some ways Cook's "Old Man" is a more powerful figure than Ruark's. For one thing, he is a composite of many woodsmen who nurtured and nour-ished the author during his development as an outdoorsman. For an-other, he touches many lives, not just one, in a poignant fashion.

The nature of that deft touch is captured in the opening lines of the foreword to Cook's first book:

> There is a quiet reverence among true woodsmen. It is as significant as changing seasons and the call of geese. Its bond is blood-like, drawing kindred spirits together from all occupations. It conquers time and omits no heart that truly understands. Those who share it, marvel at the perfection of its continuance, but become fearful of modern man's ignorance of its value.

In the present volume we see a broadening of Cook's deeply held con-victions about the importance of nature in the scheme of human af-fairs. In once sense this book is a cri de coeur, one man's heartfelt reminder to his fellow men that we neglect or forget the natural world at our own peril. On another level, it is a glowing testament to simple yet enduring truths. Most of all, though, in its pages we are constantly reminded that in the end the good earth never, ever lets us down. We can be thankful that this is a recurrent refrain, because it is one that is incapable of being overemphasized.

Geographically speaking, the good earth revealed in these pages is the soil of Tennessee, but the overriding theme, the glittering golden thread running throughout the fabric of the book, knows no limita-tions of time and place. "Bonding with the land," as Cook terms it, "that mysterious connection between man and the land," is an elusive concept that is easier to feel than to describe. You won't find it in acres of asphalt, and those minions of materialism held captive by bottom lines and profit margins likely will never savor its sweetness. Yet the bond is there for all, free for the taking.

It can be found in the sticky succulence of a frost-ripened persimmon or in a springtime dietary tonic of poke salad. Quiet, contemplative hours spent in a deer stand offer the key that opens its doors, as do the nerve-wracking moments when a lordly turkey gobbler eases his way towards seductive calls to come within gun range. Bonding is an intangible thing comprised of countless parts. It may be the whistling wings of waterfowl greeting a winter sunrise or katydids singing a tired boy to sleep after a long, lazy summer's day spent fishing. Always though, there is caring and sharing. Caring for family, friends, and the wild world which gives us sustenance. Sharing the glories of our natural heritage and the virtues it has given us as Americans—honesty, respect, courage, and a realization that the roots of our greatness spring from the soil.

All of these considerations loom large in this book, but they are not what gives it strength. Rather, it is Cook's abilities as a storyteller that make the themes near and dear to his heart (and mine) come alive. As he sings the songs of the season, for example, it is a flinty heart indeed that will remain unmoved by "Spring." Similarly, those who discern no message or meaning in "The Last Page" are sad figures, incapable of the feelings and emotions that set humankind apart from all other creatures. As an eternal optimist, though, I am convinced that anyone who reads the pages will be deeply moved.

To be taken down darkening byways into yesteryear is to walk paths of wonder, and as we tread these paths in Cook's stories we encounter signposts. These signposts remind us that we cannot know where we are going if we don't know where we've been, and they tell us that humankind came from and depends on the earth. Gladly, Cook's is not a world we have lost; sadly, it is a world we are in danger of losing.

What I am suggesting is that, along with delightful reading, there are multitudes of messages here for the discerning reader. We need to realize that that which is pure and natural is precious. We must recognize that our salvation may involve giving a corner of our soul to wild creatures. Most of all, we must remember that, while the earth is ours, we are the earth's. Cook's is a clarion call, couched in beautifully written prose, for environmental awareness. I think his words, for all that they can and should trouble you, will in the end uplift your heart. For in the final analysis this is a beautiful book, one about those aspects of human existence that are enduring and ennobling. It is with great pride I welcome this volume to the "Outdoor Tennessee" series.

Jim Casada
Series Editor
Rock Hill, South Carolina

Preface

Tennessee. I've always liked the sound of the word. Since I was a small boy, the sound of it brought a feeling of excitement and a mysterious connection with something deep inside of me. It is an uncomplicated connection, although difficult to explain in written words.

I can attempt to surround it by starting with its most definable characteristic. Tennessee is a piece of ground that has been home to my forefathers. From the mountains of East Tennessee to the Mississippi River, they have traveled before me, tasting its sweetness, the gifts of the land. Their eyes have seen, their ears heard, their hearts felt many of the same things I have also experienced. This bonding with the land by generations of family members, because it is important, is maintained through bloodlines. I remember my father's love of the land. I respected him immensely, and therefore took it in as a value worth continuing. My grandfather was the same, who told me stories of his father's land values. Everything was somehow tied to the land . . . this section of ground we call Tennessee.

Tennessee, the land, produces Tennesseans. It is no different from the soil producing an aged oak from a fallen acorn. This natural wonder, with all the greening forests, clear-running creeks, lush pastures, and productive bottomlands has sprouted us, maintained our health, and consumed us after death.

During the interim, the land has provided us with substantial obstacles to survival. Tennessee has tested us, mandated that we work hard, made us strong; and in the process, it has revealed to us that we are never strong enough to continue alone. Our survival has occurred because of our ability to join together in a unified declaration of strength through faith. To speak of Tennesseans without some reference to their faith would be incomplete.

I was raised in Tennessee, educated in Tennessee universities, and have worked for the last seventeen years as a wildlife professional. My work has taken me to virtually every county. My travels have led me to the conclusion that my family is not unique. The same land-bonds that have been strengthened in my family are to be found thousands of times throughout the land in other families. We are, therefore, bonded together as families with united values.

This book is about Tennesseans and the values they pass along. It is written straight from the heart in an attempt to reveal that mysterious connection between people and the land. Again, that powerful bond is difficult to define. It is easier found than explained.

Part I is a collection of stories about individuals. From elderly Tennesseans to youngsters, their struggles are kindred. Their values remain constant, although the conflicts are quite different. The land presents to us a wide variety of challenges, both land-born and human-made. We tend to rise to these challenges based upon our history of stubbornness, fairness, and faith. I have also attempted to give a fair representation of the land itself and the natural resources that have been given us.

Part II is three stories based upon the fictional place called Town Creek. Having spent a large part of my life in a small town on Kentucky Lake, I understand the rewards of such an upbringing. The education in spending time in such an environment is realized later in life, I think, when one has had a wealth of experience to compare. Early on, a youngster may be apprehensive whether the hometown has provided enough wisdom for the "real world." Reality, we usually find, is not so complicated after all.

Part III is a selfish endeavor. I have been recording field notes for years, both for biological data collection and personal reasons. These stories are actually reminders to myself about issues that are worthy of study, thoughts to give proper study. *Oakseeds,* for example, is an exercise in following the wandering thoughts of a deer hunter sitting patiently in his oak tree. What hunters reflect upon while in the field may be surprising to non-hunters. I have been asked hundreds of times about the source of my stories, where the ideas come from. I hope Field Notes will offer a clue.

I have been seriously blessed in my life in having had the opportunity to meet many honorable Tennesseans. They share with me their vision. They tell me of priorities. I sincerely pray my words are sufficient to fairly represent their spirits.

Part I

THE TENNESSEANS

Lost

Caroline Kenner ran fifty yards further down the hiking trail. She paused, trying to be perfectly still, so that the bird would not see her. She had run a long way from her family's campsite, playing this imaginative game with the Stellar's Jay, which was totally ignorant that it was, in the nine-year-old's mind, a handsome prince needing only a delicate touch from her hand to be set free from the wicked sorcerer's curse. The jay called once again and flew, angling this time off the main trail to a smaller game trail that led through the western sloped mountains of the Colorado Rockies. The child followed innocently, and only when the sun had fallen enough to chill the mountain air, did she forget the game and think about returning to her family.

Caroline shivered as the air quickly cooled. She ran hurriedly toward the top, but had to stop to catch her breath. The path seemed dimmer and not at all like she remembered. The trees seemed larger and the shadows had caused the mountains to change. There were no birds singing. There was no sound. The child ran again, only faster this time, until she reached a fork in the path. She stopped. The young girl could not remember this fork on her walk down the trail. The left fork led up at a sharper grade, and she knew the main hiking trail was above. Her heart beat wildly. The darkness was coming faster. She took the steeper trail for two hundred yards until in the darkened forms of a thousand towering trees and their shadows, she truly panicked. This trail is not right, she reasoned, and immediately turned back. She fell three times as she ran back toward the fork, her feet losing touch with graying trail.

Caroline Kenner missed the fork. She continued on the trail until she finally realized that she was running downhill. Confusion overwhelmed her, and she cried out for her mother, but there was no answer. She yelled again and again, but only received a blackened, silent mountain in reply. She turned and ran in the darkness, but had to slow to a walk for the fallen timber was scratching her face and arms. She had lost the trail completely and, after a long time, stumbled upon a large boulder. Climbing upon the rock she felt safer. In the distance there were water sounds from a creek, she thought. The massive rock was still warm from the day's sun, and the young girl decided to stay. The silence was overpowering and she cried softly, afraid that animals below her might hear. On the side of the mountain above her, she was sure she could hear a bear walking in her direction. Caroline Kenner lay on her side upon the hard rock bed and brought her knees against her chest, forming a tight little ball. She shut her eyes praying to Jesus for the morning to come quickly.

Mark Roby had averaged eighteen miles a day over the last week. It would take him ten days to make the circle back to his truck. Occasionally along the route, he encountered public camping areas where he would linger and visit. People were usually friendly in these areas, especially to woodsmen, who by their appearance, reflected extended trips into the back country. Mark Roby fit the part. His skin was deeply tanned by the mountain sun, and he moved as though the pack was part of him, presenting no more of a burden than his hat. He carried a hickory staff, worn smooth on both ends, and as he approached the camping area, he flicked the thinner end of the staff into the crook of his left arm, like a bird hunter cradling a shotgun.

The sun was directly overhead as he approached the camper where several people were gathered in small groups. They spoke without smiles, and Mark noticed that their voices were in quiet whispers. A large man wearing a tourist hat approached the woodsman.

"Mornin'" Mark offered.

"Hello," replied the camper. "Which direction did you come from?"

Mark Roby leaned on his staff. "South, for the last two days. Why do you ask?"

The big man paused. "There's a small girl missing since yesterday afternoon. A crew of people are out looking . . . just thought you might've seen her."

Mark knocked a dirt clod off his boot with the end of his staff. "No . . . I haven't. How old is she?"

"Nine. . . ."

"I see . . . where's she from?"

"Texas . . . I think. Yeah . . . Austin, Texas," the camper replied. "By the way, have you crossed any bears?"

The woodsmen smiled purposefully, in a direct attempt to break the tension. "I've seen a few, but try my best not to cross them. . . . Where are the parents?"

The man cast his eyes toward a dining fly behind the camper. "The mother is over there. I believe the father is still looking. It's been a long night for them."

"Thanks," Mark said, and he made his way through the people toward the awning behind the camper.

She was talking to another woman across a small table, and looked up as Mark approached. Her eyes were quite bloodshot from the tears.

"Hi, my name is Mark Roby."

She immediately stood and offered her hand. Her handshake was strong.

"Mr. Roby, I'm Katherine Kenner."

"I'm sorry to bother you, but I'm in no particular hurry," he said. "What I mean is that I have no time commitments and I'd be happy to help."

"That's very kind of you," she replied. "There are about twenty men out now."

"Could you show me the last place you saw her?" Mark asked.

"Yes . . . it's not far," she said while moving from underneath the shelter.

"We had told her she could go for a short walk and come right back. We became worried just before dark . . . she had been gone for an hour . . . and we walked the main trail for at least a mile."

"What does your husband do for a living?" Mark asked as they walked.

"He's a chemist."

"Does he spend a lot of time in the woods?"

"No," she answered. "He golfs a lot."

"Oh," Mark smiled. "When's the last time you saw him?"

"Early this morning," she replied.

"You might make sure that the Park Service is notified," he suggested. "We don't want several people lost at one time."

Katherine nodded and then stopped. "It was somewhere in here. She was on the trail up there. I remember she turned and yelled about a bird. I remember she was laughing. . . ." And Katherine Kenner had to stop talking. She wiped her eyes and tried to smile.

"I'm sorry," she whispered. "She must be so afraid out there, and I just can't stand the thought of her being alone."

"Mrs. Kenner, when I was seven years old I became badly lost. I remember the feelings. I've been lost a hundred times since then. I understand about being lost and how a child would think. If your daughter is out there, the chances are good that I will find her. Do you understand?"

Katherine Kenner nodded. "Thank you for being so sure of yourself. It helps."

"Believe me, the woods are not as large as they seem. There are only certain places your daughter would go, even if she's lost."

"May I ask where you are from, Mr. Roby? I know it's a southern accent."

Mark Roby paused. "I'm a Tennessean."

The worried mother smiled. "Somehow, for some strange reason, that helps."

"What is her name?" the woodsman asked.

"Caroline, her name is Caroline."

Mark smiled. "Call the Park Service and try not to worry. I'll be in touch."

"Thank you," she said.

Mark Roby turned and started down the main hiking trail. After five steps he turned, walking backwards.

"Does she know Zippidy-Do-Da?" he asked.

"What?" responded the mother.

"The song . . . Zippidy-Do-Da. Does she know it?"

"Yes," Katherine answered. "I'm sure she does." And the man from Tennessee disappeared from her view.

"Please . . . find her," the young mother half-yelled down the trail.

He moved slowly, trying to decipher the prints of a herd of humans as they had lumbered down the trail. Reasoning that searchers before him had yelled for her with no response, he figured that she was close to the trail and dead, or farther away, out of earshot. The timber fell off sharply to his left and ended at a sheer bluff. She could have become lost and stumbled over the edge in the dark. Easing from the trail, he angled down to the bluff and worked the edge for almost a mile. Thankfully, he found no sign and cut north until he crossed the main trail. The trail led down through a major drainage that opened into an enormous valley extending some twenty miles. Leaning against a massive boulder, he studied his map trying to unravel the mystery of the child's path. Occasionally, the fear of being lost would penetrate his thoughts. He remembered the childhood panic that had seized his heart like a monstrous nightmare choking off breaths. Mark Roby's mind flashed his own daughter, and he could feel her small arms around his neck and her hair against his face as she kissed his cheek. The woodsman pressed the staff firmly against his forehead, trying desperately to make the memories go away. Quickly, he left the boulder in route to the last place the child had been seen, like returning to the last blood sign on the trail of wounded deer.

Fifteen minutes later, he stopped. A Stellar's Jay called a hundred yards off to his left. From habit he crouched, supporting himself on the staff while he studied the ground. The trail reeked of Vibram-soled boot tracks. He glanced toward the bird sounds and immediately saw a faded game trail that would be obscured from an adult's view. His searching eyes went quickly to the ground and there, only inches from the main trail's edge, was the partial print of a small tennis shoe. Mark Roby sprang to the sign like a coyote on a field mouse. He gently moved one twig and a blade of grass from its center. It measured three fingers across. The shoe printed a series of parallel, wavy lines. He moved carefully away from the main trail for thirty yards before finding a full print in the dust. At that point, he was sure, and for the first time in almost two years, the woodsman from Tennessee was filled with an overwhelming power of enthusiasm and purpose.

He moved like a large cat, covering the ground very fast. The

sign was subtle but to the Tennessean, obvious. After finding the
fork where Caroline first became confused, within minutes he had
pinpointed her actions. He found where she fell. He found where
she returned to the fork and then where she continued in the wrong
direction. From that point, however, the tracking became intense.

On hands and knees, after a full hour, Mark finally found where
the young girl had left the game trail into the black timber. There
was no logic in her direction, and he imagined her in the dark grop-
ing for some sign of help. After a time, he found the large boulder
and little wavy marks on its side where she had climbed. He followed.
From the top of the boulder he could hear a stream below and once
again he removed the map from his pack. It then became clear to
him how the others had missed the lost child. By assuming that she
had never departed from the main hiking trail, their efforts had been
wasted on the wrong side of the mountain.

From his vantage point he could see that the terrain fell off sharply
to the stream below. Across the stream was a section of sheer bluff.
He reckoned she left the rock and made her way to the water, then
she headed downstream. He studied the boulder under his feet, and
there, under a small rim of jagged rock was one blond hair. It glis-
tened in the sunlight and moved once as a small breeze swept over
the rock. He gently reached down and freed it from the snag, knowing then that she had at least tried to sleep. If Caroline Kenner had
begun walking at first light, he was six or seven hours behind. He
must cut her off, as if working a silent, retreating gobbler back home.
He must cut her off.

The map showed a way. If the child traveled downstream, she
would make a large loop through the canyon. If he was quick enough,
and lucky, the peninsula of land within the horseshoe bend would be
traversed in a couple of hours.

Mark Roby climbed down from the rock, and without bothering
to pick up her sign, walked straight to the stream. Following the
water downstream, he had only covered a hundred yards before finding the wavy prints of her tennis shoes. Having confirmed her direction of movement, he changed course, moving upstream until he

could wade the stream and cut overland in an attempt to intersect the waterway some five miles downstream before dark.

Following his compass headings, he made surprisingly good time through the timber. There was still ample sunlight when he broke out of the timber on the north side of the peninsula. A small meadow lay on either side of the stream, and it was there that he looked carefully for any sign that she had passed before him. He worked both sides of the water for five hundred yards, but could find no child sign at all.

The Tennessean loosened his straps and let the pack fall to the stream bank. He quickly began gathering wood and within ten minutes had a cooking fire in order. He cut several large strips of fatback from his supply, and the sizzling aroma pleased him. With his hatchet, the woodsman began a deliberate chopping of the gathered wood. Its drumming echoed against the silent wilderness, much clearer than any human voices yelling a name. Over the years, he had noticed that the sounds of the camp ax carried unbelievable distances. Once while deer hunting back home in Tennessee, he listened to a farm boy splitting wood. The sounds were three ridges away, but extremely clear, and between licks he could hear the boy singing. The human voice seemed to harmonize with nature's sounds when in song.

So, he sang as he chopped firewood. He had thought hard about his choice of songs, wanting something appealing to a nine-year-old Texas girl. He figured that he could not go wrong with "The Yellow Rose of Texas," except he forgot the lyrics. So, he made some up. Then, he went into his own rendition of the "Song of the South," remembering most of those words. His voice echoed with the chopping hatchet, but his hunter's eyes remained alert for any movement.

The sun was almost gone, as was his voice. There was a sick feeling in the pit of his stomach in fear that the little girl would have to spend another night alone in the woods. He refused to consider the child being harmed. Suddenly, his eyes picked up a flicker of red, and then it was gone, like the ghost flash of a whitetail. He sang louder; it appeared again, but it did not move. Mark Roby's heart beat heavily in his chest, and he abandoned "Zippidy-Do-Da" for "The Yellow Rose." The red dot moved, bouncing lightly as it neared him.

Finally, she was there, standing ten steps away, looking skeptically into his eyes. Her red blouse was torn at the left shoulder and her once-white shorts were a mottled brown. The long, blonde hair was badly tangled, falling irregularly on her shoulders. The Tennessean grew silent and quit chopping.

"Well, hello there, Missy," he offered with a smile, controlling his urge to swoop her up, as he would have his own daughter. His throat was tight, and mysteriously his eyes were burning.

"Are you an angel?" she asked sincerely. "I prayed that an angel would find me, but you sure don't sing like an angel."

Mark Roby laughed. "No ma'am, I'm no angel, but if you are Caroline Kenner from Austin, Texas, then your Momma asked me to fetch you home. Are you ready to go home?"

And quickly the child was crying. She stood without moving, weeping unashamed, but unsure as to what to do. Within an instant, Mark was holding her, and she squeezed his neck with all her strength. He could feel the wetness from her eyes against his cheek.

"I was scared," she cried into his shoulder. He carried her to the fire and let her sit on his pack.

"It's all right . . . being alone out here can be scary to everybody. You did real good for such a little girl. I found where you slept on that big rock. That was smart."

Caroline was drying her eyes with the backs of two dirty hands.

"I was afraid they'd get me," she explained. "I heard a bear."

Mark smiled. "Well, it's all right now. We've got us a nice fire, and I'm gonna fix you some supper. Would you like some hot chocolate?"

She nodded, and he obliged, offering her a variety of meals produced from his pack. She ate enthusiastically, and in the warm firelight, he prepared his sleeping bag for her. She snuggled in the covers, using a cotton shirt for a pillow. He drank steaming hot coffee as he watched her eyes grow heavy.

"How old are you?" she whispered from the bag.

"How old do I look?" he answered.

She opened her eyes and looked at the woodsman across the fire.

"My Daddy's thirty-three. You look older than him. Maybe forty."

Mark Roby smiled. "I'm thirty-one."

"Are you sure you're not an angel?" she asked again.

"Are you sure *you're* not an angel?" he replied, but she was asleep. He watched her steady breaths in the dim light and there, beneath a million stars, the man from Tennessee felt more content than he remembered possible.

Dawn's first light found Mark Roby tending the fire. He had prepared Caroline her chocolate, steaming in a cup by the coals. He moved to the sleeping bag and gently brushed some tangled hair from her face. She shut her eyes tightly and buried her face deeper within the softness of the cotton shirt pillow.

"Rise and shine," he proposed. "Time to go home."

She briefly opened her eyes and sat upright in a child's sleeping stupor.

"Your chocolate's by the fire and *it's hot*," he preached. She promptly collapsed back into the warmth of the bag.

"Well, I guess I'll just have to throw you in the creek."

She opened one eye to study his face.

"I'm so sleepy," she moaned.

"Your parents haven't slept in two nights. . . ."

The youngster struggled to stand. Mark handed her a folded towel.

"Inside this towel is a bar of soap, toothpaste, and toilet paper. The creek is that way."

"Real toilet paper?" she asked.

"Yep, authentic Charmin," he smiled. "It doesn't take long to get priorities straight out here, does it, girl?"

"Sir?"

"Never mind, let's get clean for Momma, OK?"

"OK," she mumbled as she headed for the creek.

The woodsman broke camp and was prepared to leave when Caroline returned from the stream.

"I got everything clean except my hair," she complained. "Do you have a brush?"

"Sure do. Sit down here in front of me, and I'll see what I can do."

He produced a battered hairbrush from the pack and began gently brushing out the tangles.

"What's your name?" she asked.

"Mark Roby," he answered to the back of her head.

"I'm from Texas. . . . Where are you from?"

"Tennessee Ridge, Tennessee. Have you ever heard of it?"

She thought for a second. "I think so."

"Don't tell a story. . . ."

"Well, I've heard of Tennessee. You helped us fight the Mexicans at the Alamo."

"That's right," he laughed. "That was several years ago."

He held a lock of hair above its tangle, vigorously brushing the matted strands below his hand.

"How old is your little girl?" she asked.

Mark Roby abruptly stopped brushing. The stream sounds grew louder, and he began brushing again.

"Why do you think I have a little girl?"

"You know how to brush without hurting," she answered.

He took a deep breath. "She would have been seven this October."

"Did something happen to her?" Caroline probed.

"She and her mother were coming home from the grocery store. There was an accident."

A hawk called from high above them, cutting his words. Laying the brush aside, he smoothed her hair with his hand.

"There now . . . ," he said. "Pretty as a picture."

She stood and turned, looking him straight in the eyes. The hawk called again.

"I'm really sorry," she whispered before reaching forward and hugging his neck.

"Sometimes . . . ," he started, while gently patting her back, "you can know exactly where you are and still be lost. You've been lost for two days, and I've been lost for two years."

Caroline Kenner stepped back and smiled.

"Boy, I bet you're glad I found you."

The Tennessean laughed and the child joined in, echoing off the distant mountainside.

"C'mon," he said. "Let's go home. In three hours I'll have you hugging your Momma's neck."

Hand-in-hand they waded the shallow stream on a direct compass heading for the main trail. A Stellar's Jay cocked its head quizzically in the black timber above them as they passed below. It was probably the first time the bird had heard "The Yellow Rose of Texas" sung in perfect country harmony.

Coming Home

Tom Carson had been gone a long time. At thirty-seven, he had explored many of the land's new frontiers. Well, at least to a Tennessee boy, who grew up in the rural hills along the Cumberland River, they appeared to be frontiers. He had occasionally made it home on holidays and special anniversaries, but for the most part he had separated himself from backwoods Tennessee. He had sought the faster life that the larger cities offered and had pursued them with the enthusiasm of a beagle after a cottontail. The thickets, he noticed, were less obvious in the city, but nonetheless real and burdensome.

There was a peculiar thing about coming home. He was not sure if he had noticed it before, but the closer he got to the county line, the easier it was for him to breathe.

He relaxed his grip on the steering wheel. He eased off the accelerator. He turned off the radio. He rolled down the window.

The county line welcomed him as he passed, as did the local 4-H Club and the Oak Hills Baptist Church. Somewhere out his window he thought he heard the call of a meadowlark. At sixty miles an hour it was a bit hard to tell. The smell of home was overwhelming . . . the creek that paralleled the highway and the grass and the cattle . . . he had to stop. The car's engine idled smoothly as he stared at the pasture out his window. Stopping the engine with a turn of the key, he noticed the county's calling invading the car, and he felt the pull to get out. His legs were stiff from the four hours of driving, and the ground felt good under his feet. Crossing the road, he entered a thin patch of woods that bordered the creek, and he continued down toward the water's edge.

The creek ran clear. A redhorse scooted across the shallows toward a deep pool on the opposite bank. He remembered the days he spent along these creeks, supposedly in school, getting his own brand of education. The animals of this county and the land that produced them had provided his spirit with an adventure far exceeding anything since.

Tom looked upstream toward town and turned back toward the road. A bluegill popped a bug on the surface behind him, and he smiled, knowing the sound without having to look for confirmation.

The town square was exactly the same. Exactly the same. Stopped at one of the two red lights in town, he noticed townspeople talking on the sidewalks. They were in no hurry; just small groups talking at cars and benches, and he looked up to see that the light had changed to green. Quickly, he glanced in his rear view mirror. Instead of an enraged motorist, upset because of the unforgivable delay, his eyes met a farmer in a rusted-out Chevy truck, who casually waved as if to say, "Don't worry, I ain't in no hurry." Tom waved back and smiled.

Crossing under the second green light and passing the local funeral home on his right, he noticed a group of older men, dressed in their Sunday suits, talking on the front porch. Tom Carson wondered who had died, and his thoughts quickly returned to his last trip home. It was over a year ago, he thought. The vision of his mother was clear, smiling while she poured a cup of coffee. . . .

It was, without a doubt, the prettiest main street of any town he had ever visited. And he had visited quite a few since leaving over fifteen years ago. From New England to California, Tom had always compared the main streets of each place he visited to the sight in front of him now. Home had always won, always.

He continued west for two miles and then north, taking two more right turns. It was pure country now, with fence lines separating farms instead of houses. They were modest houses mostly, and nothing new had been constructed since his last trip home. He crossed three smaller creeks, with bridges that at one time or another in his youth had all been homes for him. Remembering words from his grandfather, who had survived the Great Depression, any place that you can build a fire and get out of the rain . . . is home. Tom hated to dispute such a learned man as his grandfather, but he reckoned the old man to be off on that bit of wisdom. Bridges could be fine homes for a ten-year-old while in the process of catching a mess of fish and as long as the bridges are in running distance of the big house. But never had a bridge pulled on his insides like the home place was pulling on his now. He slowed the car.

There was a flash in the ditch to his right as he passed a fence gate, and as much as he wanted to continue, he stopped. He walked twenty yards toward the gate, and as he approached the spot, he noticed a small boy's head in the weeds, looking down. The boy appeared to be about twelve, and he never offered to look up, but remained sitting in the weeds as the man neared from behind. Tom looked over the boy's shoulder and could see the problem, a bit lower in the undergrowth toward the fence.

The beagle lay peacefully on its left side, staring sleepy-eyed into the tall grass. There was not one mark on the dog, but Tom detected a hint of dried blood at the mouth and nose. The boy stared at the little dog, stern-faced. A patch of red extended down onto his cheeks from his eyes. His school books lay under the bicycle in the grass beside him, and Tom noticed that one book cover had been torn at the cover, just over the penciled inscription, "American History." Tom knelt beside the boy, who still had not even acknowledged an outsider's presence.

"That your beagle hound?" Tom whispered.

"Yep . . . ," answered the boy. "That there's old Hank."

Tom picked up a piece of gravel at his feet and rolled it between his fingers, trying to pick the right words.

"Well, I'm truly sorry about old Hank. It's tough losing good dogs, huh?"

The kid smiled for a split-second, and then the smile fell away.

"Hank weren't much good, mister. But he sure did think he was something, and he tried real hard." The boy wiped his nose with the back of his hand.

Tom smiled. "Well, I reckon that's the most important thing . . . tryin' hard."

The boy looked up for the first time, meeting the stranger's eyes. "I reckon that depends on whether I'm real serious about eatin' rabbits or just learnin' about dogs. Hounds that just try hard never put many rabbits in my game bag."

"Is that the main thing . . . rabbits in your coat?" Tom asked.

"Used to be . . . back when I was just startin' out, before I learned about what's what. Back when I was only ten."

"And now?" Tom continued. "Since you've got old and learned, and what about now?"

"Now . . . ?" The boy shook his head. "Now, I'm just tryin' to figure out why the more a fellow learns, the harder it is to understand."

Tom Carson tossed the gravel to the ground. "That's a tough one. What's your name?"

"Scott . . . Scott Knight. Who are you?"

"Name's Carson . . . Tom Carson, and I grew up just down the road. When I was your age, I used to run these same ridges here that you do."

Scott looked up again. "I know the Carson farm. You kin to the Carsons that used to live there, I guess."

"They were my folks," Tom whispered.

"How come I never saw you around?" the boy asked. "Me and Mr. Carson were good friends. I used to help him feed cows, back when I was ten."

"Did you? That's good. I've been gone for awhile."

"And Mrs. Carson used to fix me cheese sandwiches for helpin' her rake leaves. She was a nice lady. . . . I remember I cried when they died."

Tom looked at the kid. His eyes were big and blue, in spite of the tears old Hank had brought on. The blonde hair under his cap was short, and Tom noticed a recent briar scratch on the boy's right ear lobe.

"I cried too, Scott. We all tend to do that when we lose good folks and dogs that we real hard."

"I don't know," replied the boy. "I lost my dad two years ago. He didn't die or nothin'. Just left one day, . . . but that makes sense 'cause he was basically worthless. We're better off now. I didn't cry then."

"Well, maybe he's just trying to figure things out, like you and me and Old Hank there when he was cold trailin'."

"Maybe . . . maybe you're right, mister. You gonna stay for awhile or you just visiting?"

Tom stood up, stretching his legs again. "I've come home. I reckon I'll stick around for awhile."

"That sure is a fancy car," the boy remarked, looking up the road.

"Thanks," Tom replied. "Seeing as we're gonna be neighbors, you want a ride home? We can hide the bike in the grass and pick it up tomorrow. I reckon you'll want to take Old Hank home, anyway. Besides, I'm going to sell that fancy car real soon and buy me an old truck and a tractor, so if you want a ride, we better make it quick."

"I appreciate it. I couldn't figure out how I was gonna get Hank and my books home at the same time."

"You want me to get the dog?" Tom offered.

"No, sir. I'll get him." And the boy approached the dog, then carried him like a baby toward the car. Tom followed with the books.

They drove another half mile, the boy cradling the beagle in his lap. Tom slowed the car at the entrance to the home place. It was a long driveway and the cable was still across, preventing access to the house. He pulled into the driveway and stopped, looking at the farm-house on the hill.

The house looked sad. The absence of activity around it was too obvious and quickly he felt a lump in his throat, a pain he had long since forgotten. He turned to the boy, who was looking away, trying to hide his own pain from the passing of a friend that lay limp in his lap.

"Ain't we something?" Tom offered. "Two grown-up men sitting in a car fighting tears."

Scott turned toward his new friend and sniffed, "Yessir, but I won't tell, if you don't."

Tom smiled. "You got yourself a deal, partner. You reckon, if I get some cows, you can help me feed sometime?"

"Sure," the boy answered. "Do you hunt, mister?"

"Yes I do . . . or I did. . . . I hunt everything from bullfrogs to deer, and with the proper amount of effort, too. And I'd be proud if you'd be my huntin' partner."

The boy smiled big, letting a large tear fall to the dog's ear below. Tom looked back toward the house on the hill. He could picture the yard mowed and dogs on the porch and smoke rising from the chimney and the smell of bacon in the house and in an instant, he was happy . . . really happy, maybe for the first time in fifteen years. There was a peculiar thing about coming home. He was not sure if he had noticed it before. . . .

The Window

In 1937, Mary Shaw was twenty-two years old. In recent days, memories of her youth were more frequent, and she figured it truly amazing that the thoughts of early years could, although briefly, displace time and carry her completely away to a period when innocence was something to overcome, and thoughts of death were not yet born. She could see herself running happily through the summertime fields of home, feeling only the wind and the sun, and the cool clovered ground under her bare feet, and the smell of cut hay and cold-running creek water. . . .

Mary Shaw could see all these images in a fold in her pillow. The sun had just lightened her bedroom window, and she had awakened with these thoughts fresh on her mind. She stared straight ahead, half asleep, slipping in and out of her half-dream, returning magically to her youth. Finally, with full light, the birds outside her open window called with such intensity that she decided to get up. The pain in her back made it difficult to straighten, stiffening her briefly as her first steps were made toward the bathroom.

Before the sun had completely risen, Mary had dressed and prepared her first cup of coffee, sweetened just right with honey from her own bees. The honey had been a Godsend for her summertime allergies, as prescribed by her father more than fifty years before. She sat at the kitchen table, studying the room around her. It was not a large kitchen, but the two open windows lent to it an openness to the outside yard, making it feel larger. Alone in the house, she often contemplated the windows and walls, but would not allow herself to dwell on non-productive thoughts. Winter was the hardest, the cold keeping her inside, alone with the walls. It was then that she read, sometimes a book every three days, not allowing her time to be wasted.

She longed for the spring and summer. The gardening season was her medicine and *her* purpose. Mary Shaw's garden was a spectacle for even country folk to behold, as her lines were crisp, separating the colors and textures in an artful way, yielding her own homage to the soil, and the sun, and the rain.

A wisp of early morning wind fluttered the kitchen curtain, and she rose from the table, moving slowly toward the door. Mary paused at the window, looking out at the garden. The corn stood strong and green at the southwestern side like a protecting weather-wall for the rest of the garden. The soil was brown-black and moist-looking resembling used coffee grounds between different shades of greens. Marigolds, with their burnt-orange flowers, bordered the garden and were even interspersed between the tomatoes offering a natural insect repellent, but then, there was an out-of-place piece of brown that moved across the marigolds into a row of greasy-back beans.

Mary Shaw watched calmly as the groundhog fed, and then she slowly backed away from the window. In the corner, next to three yard sticks and a broom, stood a stock-scarred Stevens 87-A .22 rifle. The lady retrieved the gun from the corner, pulled back the bolt and released it, chambering a live round. With an arthritic thumb, she flicked the safety "on" as she moved back toward her kitchen window.

The window was already open, and Mary scooted a chair up to the sill. She removed a cushion from another chair and positioned it across the sill, making a rest for the rifle. The stock was cold against her cheek, and she had difficulty focusing her eyes on the sights and the groundhog at the same time, but she remembered her husband advising, "When your eyes go, Mary, forget about the rear sight after you're lined up. Concentrate on the front sight and the target." And she did.

The groundhog was about forty yards away, standing at the nearest corner. Mary pulled the safety rearward with her thumb, took a deep breath, released a bit of it, and began her trigger pull. She could not tell if the animal was facing her or looking the opposite direction.

The report of the old rifle was particularly loud in the house. She heard the spent brass "click" across the linoleum floor as she looked again toward the garden. It was as if the animal had mysteriously vanished. She saw nothing. Quickly, the old lady pushed the safety "on," and rested the rifle in the corner. Her eyes caught the note pad under the telephone, and among other emergency numbers was "Game Warden 733-4212." She picked up the receiver, but paused before dialing. Mary glanced at the clock above the refrigerator and quickly hung up. She reckoned it was way too early, even for game wardens.

Mary Shaw made her way onto the back porch where she collected her straw basket and hat. A roll of garden twine fell from her basket and unraveled itself across the wooden porch floor. Chasing it, she stopped its course with her foot before kneeling to pick it up, the pain in her back increasing like a toothache.

The dewed grass in the yard immediately wet her shoes as she walked slowly toward the garden. It was not like her to miss such an easy shot, she thought, but then nothing seemed to be working quite properly this entire last year—her back, her eyes, her bladder. . . .

And she saw the brown fur when only ten steps away. It lay peacefully behind the marigolds. Suddenly, without cause, Mary Shaw was saddened. She approached the stilled animal and knelt beside it, touching its back with her fingers. Mary smoothed the reddish hair before turning it over. Its eyes were closed and there was a green leaf barely protruding from its mouth. Below the heart was one drop of blood, blazing red against the thinning breast hair.

Somewhere behind her she heard tires on gravel and a door slam shut, and mysteriously there was a hand on her shoulder, but she could not look up.

"What's wrong, Mary? Are you all right?"

Mary Shaw turned and looked up into the face of the younger game warden. She saw his truck and boat parked out on the road in front of her house. The big man smiled as he saw her wet eyes.

"You look a mess," she offered, "When's the last time you slept?"

"A while back," he smiled. "Are you OK?"

"Yeah," she said. "Just a bit confused in my old age. I bet I've killed fifty groundhogs in my gardens over the years. Never regretted any of their deaths, but for some reason this one seems wrong. . . . How come you're out this way so early?"

The game warden sat in the wet grass. He smelled like fish. "Oh, we finally caught those illegal netters last night out on the lake. I'm just on my way home and saw you out here, and you were so still. . . ."

She looked back at the groundhog. "I remember the first groundhog I ever did see shot. It hurt me then, too. Daddy shot it out of the sweet potatoes. I couldn't understand why he had to shoot it."

He chewed on a piece of grass. "So why's this one different, Mary?"

"I don't rightly know," she offered. "Except, I all of a sudden-like saw that me and this old groundhog have a lot in common. He surely loves the ground more than most animals, and I do so, too. I don't know what I would do if'n I couldn't work the ground. And there's enough for both of us, for sure 'cause I always grow far too much. And, well, this was his last garden, and you can't never tell—it may be mine too."

The game warden repositioned himself in the grass, lying on his right side, his head propped up with his right hand.

"Might be, Mary. This may be my last day in the woods, but it's not good to tarry on those kinds of thoughts."

"You smell like fish," she kidded.

"Yes'm . . . I certainly do. Goes with the work," he laughed.

"Did I ever tell you," she began, "how much I appreciate you. . . ."

He smiled at her. "Not in words, Mary, but I know. . . ."

"Shut up," she said. "I would like to finish this 'cause I'm afraid the mood may never strike me again."

"Yes ma'am."

"You never patronized me as an old lady," she said. "I hate that—and you never did. You are the only friend I have that I can talk to about the ground and birds and plants, and it's not for show—not for just the thought of being nice to an old lady."

The game warden laughed. "I ain't gonna let you get away with nothin', Mary. Age don't mean nothin' to me. Besides, sometimes I feel *real* old."

"So tell me, Mr. College boy, how come I have this sudden sadness about this animal. You tell me your theory. . . ."

The man yawned and shut his eyes. "You got any coffee, Mary? I'm suddenly so sleepy—I haven't slept in two days."

"Well," she said. "It looks like I'll have to pour some down you just to get an answer." Mary Shaw got to her feet and started toward the house.

The game warden smiled. "Hey," he yelled. "Don't you patronize me. . . . You know the answer."

"We are all the same, Mary. Everyone of us who has ever breathed a breath or tasted water; we're all the same. We're all one in the same . . . whether we live in holes or trees or houses. We're all part of this great big, wonderful plan, . . . and it's painful when some leave before the others."

"Did they teach you that in college?" she asked.

"No," he smiled. "Groundhogs in Mary Shaw's gardens taught me that. . . ."

Mary Shaw returned with the coffee to find the game warden asleep in the grass. She laid the tray on the ground and kneeled beside him. His head was only inches from the fallen groundhog, and she found a peacefulness in her garden that she had never before known. There were dried fish scales on his sun-tanned arms, and his uniform shirt was stained with blood and fish slime, and yet, asleep in the grass at the edge of her marigolds, he seemed so clean—like the brown-black soil that healed her aching hands as she worked her ground.

Grit

Kathryn Saunders sat cross-legged on the rug in front of the fireplace. Her eyes were transfixed on the flames, and she blinked not when small explosions of crackling gases showered sparks across the logs. The warmth on her face was comforting, allowing her thoughts to drift lazily through the flames.

She was thirty-two, single, and entirely happy living alone. She had retired from city life last year, returning to her childhood home in the Tennessee countryside. Her memories of this house, this farm— had very suddenly overpowered her desire for a continued city-borne success, and after her mother's recent death, Kathryn had come home. The loss of her parents was difficult, for the family had been extremely close; the silence of the empty house was deafening, forcing her to stay busy. She had fifteen chickens, twenty-one head of Hereford cows, four cats, two dogs, a well-stocked pantry and an adequate supply of reading materials. Her bank account was dwindling, but as she readjusted to country life, so did her need for money. Priorities seemed to be falling in place, and she was content in her efforts to establish herself on the farm, or maybe *find* herself would be more truthful, she thought. Kathryn had no visions of forever farming; she took each day on its own merit. Perhaps, she reckoned, as she sipped her coffee, there could be a continuance of her painting, and she could combine the two loves of her life—painting and living close to the land.

Kathryn Saunders smiled into the fire when thinking of her image in the community. These were all good people, hard working and compassionate; however, they could not quite grasp the idea of Kathryn returning from Houston to become a farmer. Pretty girls don't have muddy boots. Successful ladies don't enjoy driving dented pickup trucks. Intelligent women, who *could* escape from the country and *actually did*, were crazy to ever return. These wonderful people accepted Kathryn, but considered her a bit strange, . . . and she loved them for their truthfulness, but far more than any other reason, Kathryn loved home for its uncomplicated priorities . . . hard work, enthusiastic play, and unbashful thanksgiving.

She stood from her sitting position, both knees popping as she straightened. The antique clock ticked loudly on the mantle, drawing her attention to the framed picture of her parents. They were younger then, and both were laughing. The mother looked anything but motherly as she hugged the big man's neck. It was summertime, she figured, remembering the hanging ferns on the front porch above the swing where they sat. Kathryn smiled at her parents in the photo, and quickly turned toward the window where dawn's first light grayed the blackness.

The old farmhouse was a wonderfully cozy place to be in predawn April. The mornings were winter-like, adding pleasure to the crackling fires in the den, but the day progressed to full-fledged spring with all its glory and newness. Never before, however, had Kathryn known the true heralder of spring . . . the monarch of spring's majesty, and never before had she enjoyed the frame of mind to appreciate his gift. Collecting a coat from the rack, she opened the front door and made her way to the porch swing where forty years before her parents had laughed before having their picture taken. The swing was cold against her backside, and the chain squeaked as she moved. She looked across the yard and gravel road toward the tree line some two hundred yards away. It lay outstretched against the creek, below the bluff that made a large circle around a good portion of her farm. The owls had just started, and she had not heard the first cardinal.

Ten minutes later when the sky was truly lighter, the turkey sounded. His gobble ricocheted off the bluff and echoed across the pasture. Kathryn smiled and snuggled deeper into the fleeced collar of her coat. It excited her heart to know that such wild sounds were born on her land. Another turkey answered from across the pasture, and she laughed out loud at the competition between the two birds. And so, alone on her porch swing on a cold April morning, Kathryn Saunders welcomed a new day by slowly swinging and listening to turkey gobblers vying for female attention across the pasture.

The shot was muffled but loud. Kathryn quickly tried to pinpoint its location, but with the echoes off the bluff, it was difficult to be sure. She ran into the house, grabbed a .45 automatic from her bedside table, along with an extra clip, wedged the pistol expertly between her jeans and the small of her back, and was out on the gravel road running toward the shot within forty-five seconds. After two hundred yards, she found an old Chevrolet truck hidden in a cane thicket. She followed a foot path behind the truck leading toward the bluff, and after finding fresh tracks in the sand, she quickly hid behind an oak blowdown beside the path. She did not have to wait very long.

He came at a run, carrying the dead turkey over his back, its wings flopping in cadence with his steps. Kathryn heard him a full second before he became visible on the footpath, and she was surprised at her lack of fear. She was enraged. When ten feet away, she emerged from the blowdown blocking his path. The poacher stopped abruptly, and Kathryn noticed that blood was dripping from the beak of the dead turkey onto the back of his leg.

"You are on my property," she said calmly.

"Yes'm," the bearded man smiled. "And if you'll just step out of my way, I'll be off your property real quick like."

"You are on my property without permission," she repeated. "That's against the law,"

"Ma'am, get out of my way."

"You listen to me, Mister," she ordered. "You're on *my* land. Don't you tell *me* to get out of *your* way."

But he was walking toward her. "I said move, lady. . . . I don't want to hurt you."

Kathryn Saunders pulled the .45, thumb-cocked it, and pointed it squarely at his head. Her voice quivered as she whispered.

"I will blow your head clean off . . . lay the shotgun down very slowly . . . keep the muzzle away from me. . . ."

The turkey poacher obliged. The dark hole in the end of the .45 followed his eyes as he kneeled to lay down the shotgun.

"You are under arrest . . . citizens arrest," she said. "Leave the gun."

She stepped from the path so he could pass. "Hold the turkey in front of you with both hands," she ordered. "Let's go."

He held the turkey outstretched in front of him as she had ordered, and passed her on the path.

"That's a hen," she said. He remained silent. "Not only are you a trespassing poacher, but a *hen killer!*" Kathryn followed him from the woods.

As they neared the truck, he spoke for the first time since their confrontation.

"Lady, I'm gonna get in my truck and leave. If you want to kill me . . . you better get ready 'cause I'm leavin'." He tossed the turkey in the bed of the truck and reached to open the door.

Kathryn Saunders very calmly shot the left rear tire of the old truck, and then proceeded to shoot every other tire. The turkey bushwhacker was shaking, never taking his eyes from the girl with the gun.

"Pick the turkey up," she ordered.

"Yes, Ma'am," he replied. She popped the clip on the .45, and replaced it with a fresh one.

"Let's go for a walk," she commanded. And in single file, the farm girl with the .45 followed the camouflaged-clad turkey poacher down the middle of the country road. She noticed that it was suddenly no longer cold, but that spring had taken over, and there was a freshness in the air.

After a quarter of a mile they came to the next farmhouse. An older man in bib overalls was at the mailbox. His eyes followed the pair as they approached him.

"What have you got yourself, little girl?" asked the farmer.

Kathryn smiled, "Could you help me out a bit, Henry, and see if you can contact the local wildlife officer and tell him that I have a no-good, hen-killing, turkey poacher for him."

Henry walked to the road and circled the man holding the turkey.

"Kathryn, what kind of man would kill a hen turkey?" Kathryn smiled and Henry continued. "I bet he beats his children, too." Henry spat into the road and headed toward the house.

Within ten minutes, seven turkey hunters had converged in Henry's yard. It seems that the old farmer had made a few more phone calls. They held a meeting over the hood of Slim McIntosh's Ford Bronco and elected Tom Wilson as their spokesman. Tom was known county-wide for his cool delivery and meaningful expressions. He left the group and walked respectively toward Kathryn Saunders who was sitting on the tailgate of Henry's pickup truck, still holding the .45.

"Ma'am, my name is Tom Wilson and I own the farm about a mile down the road. I've heard a lot about you, but have not had the privilege of meeting you. There are several of us who would like you to know that this man, no, this thing is not a turkey hunter, and we are forever in your debt for catching him. You see, ma'am, there is nothing lower than a hen killer . . . nothing . . . and I would like permission to have a few words with your prisoner before the game warden gets here."

Kathryn smiled, "I appreciate your thoughts, and you have my permission to talk to this man. But, be good."

Tom walked over to the bearded man who was still holding the hen turkey outstretched in front of him. He stood flat-footed and looked the poacher straight in the eye. Tom spoke in a deliberate whisper with a seriousness that demanded attention.

"Who are you, fella?"

"I ain't saying nothin'," replied the poacher.

"Okay . . . then you better listen real good. We don't cotton to hen killers around here. As a matter of fact, you're extremely lucky to be gettin' off with what you're going to get. But, what I want you to *completely* understand is that if you have even thought bad things about this lady . . . if you have *any* plans of revenge, forget them. If any harm comes to this lady or her property, I will personally hunt you down like the dirty dog that you are and break your neck. Do you understand?"

The poacher nodded without speaking.

Tom continued, "Listen to me, *do you understand?*"

"Yes."

"Good." And the turkey hunter walked back toward Kathryn. He tipped his hat as he spoke.

"You got grit, lady, and we're all obliged. If there's anything we can do to help you out, please let us know. You have a nice day now."

Kathryn Saunders watched the man walk away. She found a wonderful significance in Tom Wilson's approval. It was a simple, honorable display of friendship. She was not accustomed to such uncomplicated pleasure. She hoped that some day he might take her turkey hunting although she was not sure about the killing. She was sure, however, that the attraction to wild things was an honorable thing if done in an honorable way. She was not sure of many things, but she was learning. . . .

Trajectories

In June of 1874, a young buffalo hunter named Billy Dixon purposefully shot an Indian off a horse at an estimated range of 1,538 yards. This famous shot occurred at the conclusion of the Second Battle of Adobe Walls in the Texas Panhandle after a group of Comanche, Kiowa, and Arapaho made war on a trading post occupied by a few traders and hunters. Billy Dixon used a Sharps rifle which propelled a 465-grain bullet at an estimated velocity of 1,320 feet per second. The shot was amazing, perhaps the greatest long range shot with open sights in the history of American warfare. Whether Billy could have duplicated his shot, proving his alleged skill, is open to speculation.

Such speculation prompted the formation of the "Billy Dixon Research Society" in Tennessee. The society had three members, all retired from successful avocations and dedicated to the duplication of Mr. Dixon's shot. Their interest had nothing to do with the conflict itself or the principles involved, but only in the trajectory of the shot and whether or not the incident was reported truthfully. Since their interest was semi-competitive, each hoping to be the first to duplicate the shot, they decided that all the rifles should be exactly the same, like stock car racing where the difference is in the drivers not the cars. They ordered three identical Sharps rifles from Big Timber, Montana, complete with express barrels and Creedmore sights.

Doctor Mitchell Hatchet was the unofficial leader of the trio, although Elijah Forrest would take exception with Doc's leadership skills. Ben Gaines, the third member of the group, would smile at such an observation, simply stating, "Whatever winds your watches, boys."

When the rifles arrived, they were inspected with the scrutiny of over a hundred years of combined riflemen's knowledge. The guns were, in fact, quite identical, even when one compared the grain in the walnut stocks. Wood to metal fit was excellent, the bluing deep and lustrous. The actions were smooth and the triggers exceptional, but the segregation of pieces to society members took five days of bickering to resolve.

"This one feels heavier, don't you think, Doc?" Eli asked.

"No."

"Well, feel her, Doc," offering the rifle with an outstretched hand. "This'un feels a bit more weighty."

"I felt her, Eli! For five days I've been feeling her! Ask Ben. He'll tell you. They are all the same!"

Ben smiled, peeling an apple with his Case. The green rind hung from the fruit in a spiraling coil.

"I figure if I wait long enough, you two will get mad enough to kill each other. Then I'll get all three."

So, they finally drew straws, Ben getting the first choice, and Doc the second. Eli grabbed the remaining rifle and lifted it.

"I knew it! The weightier one!" he complained.

In the two months since the rifles arrived, the famous Billy Dixon shot had not yet been duplicated. They established the testing ground in a long creek bottom on Hanging Tree Ranch where Ben Gaines ran his horses. Building the shooting bench under a big oak tree, they then marked off 1,500 yards, almost a mile away, and erected a suspended steel gong measuring two feet by three feet. Behind the target they built a plywood background and painted it white, simulating the 1874 sky. Without it, seeing the gong was nearly impossible.

They met once a week, whenever the weather was tolerable. Alternate targets providing the majority of their shooting action were constructed at closer ranges up to five hundred yards. At the conclusion of each session, each member was allowed one shot at the long range gong. The others watched with high power spotting scopes for a hit.

They concluded after the first month of shooting that Billy Dixon was either the luckiest shooter that had ever lived or that the whole passel of witnesses were bald-face liars.

"How do we know that feller didn't just drop off his horse from a heart attack? Good fights'll do that sometimes, you know, give heart attacks," Eli pondered out loud.

"It's documented!" Doc blurted. "It's in the literature."

"So!" Eli argued. "Literatures don't always tell the truth!"

Eli eased over to Ben's chair while Doc adjusted his Creedmore. He whispered.

"What's the literature?"

"It's a book of famous rifle shots," Ben whispered back.

"Who wrote it?"

"Feller named Matthew Quigley."

Eli looked stunned. "The one in the movie?"

"Yeah," Ben smiled.

"He's real?" Eli raised his eyebrows.

"What are y'all whispering about back there?" Doc asked loudly.

"Eli's confused about your reference to literature."

"I'll say," Doc said without looking up. "Confused is a flattering term to describe Eli's condition."

"Oh yeah . . . well, I'll tell you something Mister Doctor Hatchet. You never could doctor worth a flip. I only gave you my business because I felt sorry for you," Eli said pointing his finger.

"That right? Well, I'll tell you something, Eli. You are a card carrying hypochondriac. If I had a dollar for every disease you thought you had contracted, I'd be rich."

"But you are rich, Doc," Ben smiled.

"Me! What about you? I never did understand how a man could make a living selling horses," Doc continued.

"That's easy, Mitchell. I raise good horses."

"Let's shoot," Doc stated, ending the conversation. He bedded the heavy rifle in the sand bags and adjusted his seat at the bench. A large man, a bit overweight, he still had the air of a doctor. Ben could see the back of his bald head through the mesh ball cap as Doc thumb-cocked the Sharps. Click, click.

Eli spotted from the observation table, his right eye buried in the scope. Ben shifted his attention to him and marveled at the man's fitness for his age. A retired game warden, Elijah Forrest was the epitome of country smart. A newcomer would probably think Eli mentally slow, or even impaired, but that was exactly the way Eli wanted it. In his day, Eli had made hundreds of wildlife violation convictions based upon that one tactic, camouflaged intelligence. In reality, Ben figured his red-headed friend to be one of the smartest men he had ever known.

The Sharps roared. They listened, not really knowing if a hit could be heard at such a distance.

"Well?" Doc asked.

"No," Eli said.

"No, what? Could you see where I hit, any dirt or anything?" Doc pouted.

"Ben, come here and spot," Doc ordered. "He wouldn't tell me if I got close."

"I don't understand something," Eli announced to the air in front of him. Doc rolled his eyes, throwing his hands in the air.

"How come our target is only two by three feet? What was Dixon shooting at, pygmy Indians? I'll bet they rode Shetland ponies, too."

"Torso measurements, Eli," Doc explained. "The size of a man's torso."

"Well, what's wrong with arms and legs and heads and stuff?"

Ben grabbed his Sharps and moved to the bench. Doc finished logging his last shot holdover in a notebook.

"Eli," he said. "We haven't hit the backdrop yet. The problem is your shooting, not the target size."

Ben dropped a cigar-sized shell into the chamber and closed the action. He was a tall, lanky man who always wore western boots, faded jeans, and a long-sleeved white shirt, buttoned at the wrists.

"Watch real close, Eli," he said, moving into shooting position. "I'm working a new trajectory."

"Raising it up a bit?" Eli pried.

"I'll not rise to that bait," Ben smiled, recognizing the hidden subtleness of Eli's question.

Doc occupied the vacant scope, assisting in the spotting of Ben's shot. They could hear the horseman take a deep breath and release it, cheek on walnut, finger on the set trigger. Soft click. The wind flag was motionless at the bench. BOOM!

Ben recovered from the shot and looked at his friends. Doc looked at Eli. Eli looked back.

"I don't know. I've got a feeling," Eli said.

"Me, too. Let's go look," Doc agreed.

The Bronco bounced across the field, nearing the target. They parked and walked the last ten steps. The bullet hole stood out on the plywood like a fly on a piece of paper. It was low by two feet and a tad to the right, splintering the back of the wood backdrop.

"We really don't know if that was Ben's shot or mine," Doc offered scientifically.

"I do," said Eli. "You hit a football field in front of the target. I was gonna tell you later, Doc."

Doc swung at Eli with his cap, the old game warden laughing as he retreated. Ben Gaines studied the big hole in the wood.

"Next week, boys," he predicted.

"Only my Roy could shoot a coyote that far," Eli laughed.

Doc found humor in that. "C'mon, Roy," he continued the script, "tell us the secret of your near success."

Ben thought carefully about sharing his information. He knew they had both figured carefully on bullet weights, velocities, and projected bullet drop over the 1,538 yards.

"I'll tell you what, boys. Let's play a little game here. Everybody take your pen and write on your hand how many feet you reckon that bullet will drop. We'll open at the same time."

They separated, each man scribbling in the palm of his hand. Turning, they extended their hands, knuckles almost touching.

"Turn," Ben said.

They opened, exposing their personal calculations on the bullet drop of their guns. Doc's hand read "320 feet." Ben's palm said "a hair over a football field." Eli's figure was legible under yellowed calluses. It read "318.65 feet."

"Ain't that interesting?" Ben asked.

"Sure is," Doc said. "What is this, point six five stuff, Eli? How'd you figure that? I don't think you can add, much less perform mathematical calculations."

"Oh, I can't, Doc. I stopped by the college. Old Hank, you know, the math department head, I trapped some beaver for him last year, and, well, he ran a computer program for me."

"Right," Doc said.

Ben smiled and turned, walking back to the Bronco.

"Wait a second, Ben," Eli yelled. "What's the difference here. We all know the answer."

Ben opened the door and looked back.

"Knowing the answer, boys, ain't necessarily enough."

A week later, Ben Gaines's Bronco was parked under the big oak when Doc and Eli arrived. Ben sat in his lawn chair, staring at the distant target, the Sharps across his lap. He didn't greet his friends, but they just figured he was concentrating on the shot.

"You better not have snuck down here and practiced without us, Ben," Eli said approaching the bench.

Ben smiled at Eli. "I don't do much sneakin'."

Doc laid his gear on the bench, finally pulling a Thermos and three cups from his bag. He poured the steaming brew and delivered Ben his cup.

"You ready to perform a famous shot?"

"Thanks, Doc."

"You know, boys, I've been thinking about trajectories," Doc started. He sat on the bench and motioned with his hand. "It's strange how our lives are like the path of these bullets. We start out young and fast, feeling the explosion of life. Then, the farther we go, we rise to where we are the most productive, middle aged, when we have that brief combination of knowledge, experience, and energy. But then, we start getting old, like us, and the bullet falls off real fast getting slower and slower until. . . ."

"I have a cancer," Ben announced calmly.

There was an uncomfortable silence as Doc's smile fell. Eli looked down, unable to keep Ben's eye, thinking he heard a red-tailed hawk scream somewhere behind him.

"Where?" Doc asked.

"Prostate."

"How come you didn't come to me first, Ben?"

"You're retired, Doc," Ben smiled. "Besides, you're more my friend that my doctor."

"How advanced is it? I mean, we've probably all got a touch of it. Old timers generally do."

Ben sipped his coffee. "It's . . . it's more than a touch, Mitchell."

Eli tried to speak, but his voice broke, and he purposefully coughed to cover it up.

"This coffee's terrible, Doc," he lied.

Ben Gaines stood, stretching his six foot five frame. He moved to the bench, broke down the Sharps action and dropped a cartridge in the chamber. It rattled before seating home. He closed the action.

"Y'all spot for me. I'm ready to shoot."

After steadying his rifle on the bags, he took aim. They heard the hammer cock.

"I told you because you are my friends. I don't keep things from my friends. Besides, I'd hate if you heard it from somebody else," he said.

They watched him, his head above the stock, talking to them like it was part of the shooting process.

". . . but, I'd appreciate us just forgetting the whole thing. I've got some time left. I'd hate if it got tainted with worry." He paused. "Done?"

"Done," Doc nodded.

Ben looked to Eli. Eli smiled. "Ben, you gonna jabber all day or shoot that pygmy target?"

He checked the wind. None. He felt the stock against his cheek. Set the trigger. Inhale. Let some out. Concentrate. BOOM!

They watched the target through the high magnification optics. Two seconds. Three seconds. Four seconds. Almost five seconds after the bullet left its birthing bore, it had risen ninety-five feet above the sight line, and then aged, dropping quickly toward its end. It slammed into the steel target, cratering the steel and knocking black paint from its surface. The steel swung violently backwards on its suspended chains, back and forth, clearly visible to the spotters.

They looked at Ben. He looked back at them, offering that soft-spoken smile.

"Well, boys?"

"Steel's swingin'," Eli smiled.

"That's some fine shooting, Partner," Doc said as he offered his hand to Ben. The horseman took it and then Eli's. He picked up the Sharps and ejected the spent brass. It hit the table and rolled.

"We're all good shooters, Doc. I just found the target first. Just so we find the target. That's the thing. Now, who's next?"

Uprooted

It is a long way from Del Rio, Tennessee, to Belleville, Illinois. When seventeen and the mountains of Appalachia have always been home, Illinois is not necessarily "greener pastures," regardless of your father's business advancement. Besides, John Bible figured, how could any move be beneficial if a man can not understand the dialect of its inhabitants? For sure, he would never understand the fast-talking Northerners, and he reckoned there was not enough time left in his life to teach these people proper diction.

John drove the old truck slowly through the snow, passing field after field of harvested corn. He strained his eyes to see a blemish on the flat land, some kinship to a hill, but there was none. He badly missed the mountains after only one week, so much in fact, that an agonizing emptiness would occasionally overwhelm him. He glanced at his younger brother, who sat quietly by the window, staring uninterestingly ahead.

"What are you studying about so hard?" asked John.

Tom Bible paused before answering. "This stinks . . . the whole thing really stinks. What's so good about this place?"

John thought as he watched the big flakes start up again and crash nonviolently against the windshield.

"Well," he started. "It's a nicer house. Your room is much larger."

"Oh well," countered the younger bother. "That's a good reason to leave home. Why don't we just move to Bolivia or Argentina or . . . Brazil. We could probably afford a mansion down there if that's the best reason you can think of."

"You sweet on South America or something," smiled John Bible. "What's this 'Bolivia' stuff?"

Tom spoke to his window. "At least it's south."

They drove for five miles before turning into the parking lot of the high school. It was a large school with hundreds of parked cars. There were students milling around the cars and assembling toward the front entrance like re-grouping quail. John found an empty slot and eased the old truck to a stop.

"You nervous?" he asked.

Tom made no attempt to open the door.

"I ain't taking nothin'. They better leave me alone."

John smiled. "Ease up, little brother. We're gonna have to take a little ribbin'. You remember how it was when new people moved to our school. Smile at 'em . . . don't let them get to you. We'll find some good people along with the bad."

Tom Bible looked at his brother. "I'll try . . . but this really stinks. I want to go home."

John sighed. "Me too, but we've got to make the best out of it. First day's always the worst, but just in case . . . let no man lay hands on you. That's the law."

They made their way through the masses toward the main office. It was peculiar, John thought, that the school smelled exactly the same as school back home. Every high school in the entire U.S.A. must smell the same, he reckoned. The droning voices mixed with slamming locker doors were overcome with erratic singular yells or screams. The brothers eased through the crowd, noticing a hundred lingering glances from all directions. There were giggles from a small covey of girls at a water fountain, and John noticed the back of his brother's neck was blood red around the collar of the blue flannel shirt.

The bell was extremely loud. Tom jumped when it went off and then gave his brother an embarrassed smile. The halls were quickly empty, and for the first time John could tell that the floors were cleanly polished. Somewhere down a distant, darkened hall was the gym, for both could hear a single bouncing basketball and its deliberate echoes.

After checking in at the office, the Bible brothers re-emerged into the silent halls with their respective room assignments. John paused at the trophy case.

"Hey," he whispered.

"What?"

"You hang in there, little brother. This ain't nothin'. I mean . . . it's not like we're fixin' to get field dressed."

Tom smiled. "You watch your backtrail, John." And they separated, each taking a lonely hall to himself, like parting at a fork on an East Tennessee mountain trail.

John could not figure whether the classes were more formal than at home, or the difference was in the people themselves. At any rate, he was not totally lost. He kept to himself, taking good notes and trying to catch up on reading assignments. He found that people were genuinely interested in the Tennesseans, but could not yet decipher why. John Bible made it through lunch without a hitch.

He had eaten quickly, leaving twenty minutes of free time before
the next class. While exploring the gym, a door at the far end of the
floor opened briefly allowing the commotion from outside to filter
in, along with two burly looking boys with long hair. John Bible
began a deliberate walk down the side of the bleachers meeting the
two strangers at mid-court. They whispered to each other as they
approached and blocked his path attempting to force his route onto
the court, but John did not move.

"Where do you think you're going?" asked the smaller of the two.

John smiled. "Oh, I just figured I'd see what all the commotion's
about."

The bigger boy snickered. "He's a figurin' . . . is that some of
that hick Tennessee talk, boy?"

John stopped smiling. "No . . . now move out of my way."

"Why? So you can go out there and get kicked like your brother?"

"Move," said the Tennessean.

"How would you like to make us, mountain boy?"

Quickly John answered. "How would you like to die?"

They paused and then nervously separated, allowing the Tennessean to pass, but they followed closely behind.

John found his brother in a fighting position, fists clenched tightly
in front of his face. There was blood under his nose, and his shirt was
torn at the right shoulder. A half dozen on-lookers were gathered in
a taunting semi-circle around the fighters. Tom's opponent was five
inches taller and thirty pounds heavier. John never hesitated, but
walked calmly between them, and pushed the older fighter away with
a firm right arm.

"Back off," he commanded and quickly the fighter swung.

John stepped back, allowing the punch to narrowly miss his nose,
and instinctively he threw a straight, right hand that centered the
fighter's face. The force of the blow was impressive, as was the sight
of the unconscious form crumpling in the snow.

"OK," John Bible said as he faced the crowd. "Who's next? Huh,
c'mon boys, let's get this over with. Anybody wonderin' about what

us Tennessee boys have got can find out right now. C'mon, don't be
bashful. . . ."

An acne-scarred native stepped forward with his right hand hidden
in his jacket pocket. He raised the pocket as he spoke.

"How 'bout I just cut your throat? How 'bout that, tough boy?"

And suddenly, John Bible felt the rage boiling in his veins. He
moved forward toward the thug.

"Pull it, punk . . . pull it out . . . but you better kill me 'cause if
anything comes out of that pocket except your fingernails, so help
me, I'll gut shoot you with a dull broadhead and you won't hear
nothin' 'ceptin the whistle of the arrow . . . pull it. . . ."

The punk's eye twitched as they stood toe to toe. He tried to
smile, but the corners of his mouth trembled too badly.

"Later . . . Tennessee boy . . . I'll see you later. . . ."

And they moved away, leaving the brothers from Del Rio alone
in the snow.

"Are you all right?" John asked.

"Yeah," Tom answered. "He sucker punched me."

"What started it?"

"I don't know. One of them was going to show me his car, and
when I got outside they were already there and started in on me.
The big one that you pole-axed hit me when I turned around."

John smiled. "C'mon, little brother. It's better we got it over
with early." And the Bible brothers walked shoulder to shoulder
back into the gym.

After the last bell, they met at the front water fountain, as planned.
They reckoned it would be a tad safer to make the walk to the old
Ford together. Once outside, they immediately noticed two forms at
the truck.

"Well," John said as they walked. "Looks like we got company."

"At least the odds are better than at lunch," Tom answered.

"Let's split at the truck . . . you go one way and I'll take the other.
We'll have 'em hemmed up between us."

"OK, Tom agreed.

At the truck, the two students smiled at the approach of the brothers from Tennessee.

One held up his hand as he leaned on the tailgate.

"Peace," he laughed. "My name is Jim Gerber. This is my brother Paul."

John Bible noticed their dress was more like their own. They were faded jeans and boots. One wore a camouflaged jacket.

"Pleased to meet you. Sorry if we come off kind of defensive, but it hasn't been a real good day," John said.

"We heard," smiled the smaller brother. "Don't worry about that bunch. It's better you confronted them early. From what we heard, they won't be bothering you anymore. You broke Fisher's nose, if you hadn't heard."

"Real sorry to hear that," said John.

"Anyway," continued Jim Gerber, "We heard about the dull broadhead and wondered if, in fact, you really shoot. We shoot all the time and bow hunt on the weekends and, well, we're having a club rabbit hunt this Saturday. Just wondered if you're interested."

Tom Bible smiled at his brother. "John here is the Robin Hood of the family, but I'd love to go and carry the rabbits."

John smiled. "That is the nicest thing that's happened all day. We'd love to come." And the four hunters shook hands at the back of the truck.

They met at the club archery range on the following Saturday morning. When the Tennesseans arrived, there were four hunters already practicing. The Gerber brothers waved, and John retrieved his bow and quiver from the back of the truck. As they approached the targets, the archers stopped, looking curiously at John Bible's bow.

"Mornin'," John greeted.

"Hello," answered the four hunters, and Tom noticed the fartherest two shooters were whispering to themselves.

Jim Gerber smiled. "It's been awhile since I've seen one of those."

The Tennessean withdrew the longbow from its cloth case and began the stringing procedure. One of the other hunters laughed out loud and asked, "Does everybody in Tennessee shoot those things? Hasn't the news got out about compounds?"

John smiled. "No and yes."

Paul Gerber cast a glance at his Illinois friends. "You're showing your ignorance . . . I've never seen a longbow shooter yet who wasn't good. I'll bet you ten bucks he can beat you. . . ."

The bowhunter laughed. "That's a bet. What range would you like to shoot, Mr. Bible?"

"All of them," John said, as he slung the back quiver into position, allowing the two dozen cedar shafts to rattle briefly. "One shot at each target . . . one arrow."

"What's it pull?" asked Jim Gerber.

"Seventy pounds at twenty-eight inches," answered John. "It takes some getting used to."

"What's that wood?" asked another.

"Laminated horse apple," John replied.

And the others were laughing.

"Horse apple?" they questioned. "What's horse apple?"

"You know," Tom said. "Horse apple, bodock, osage orange."

As they laughed, John Bible prepared the first arrow. He withdrew it from the quiver and slid it expertly across the primitive rest until it came home on the string. There was a fox target on the first backstop.

"Call the shot, Tom," John whispered and Tom replied.

"Neck shot."

And the arrow was quickly gone. It was almost too fast to see, but the white fletching quivered in the neck of the red fox. A bobcat target was on the thirty yard backstop, and Tom called for a lung shot. At his words, the arrow was gone, thudding perfectly behind the front shoulder. The buck target was at forty yards, standing broadside looking toward the hunters.

"Right ear," Tom laughed. The others were silent, watching awestruck at the archer's precision.

John pulled smoothly and when his right hand reached the anchor point, the arrow was gone. It whistled in flight and punched a clean hole in the right ear of the buck. He lowered his horse apple bow and smiled.

"Just lucky, I guess."

The bowhunter shook his head.

"No contest, friend. That's the finest shooting I've ever seen. You're all right, John Bible.

"Thanks," he replied.

"How do you do that without sight pins? I've never understood instinctive shooters."

"Heck," John said. "A good quarterback doesn't have sight pins. He practices hard and throws good passes. I just throw arrows."

So, the Bible brothers from Del Rio, Tennessee, took out to the corn fields of Illinois with four new friends. They found that the same stirrings of the heart are found tracking snow bound cottontails in Illinois, as well as in Tennessee. They found that man's bonding with the land is universal, like the smell of high school halls, but the aching to return home never leaves . . . especially for Tennesseans reared in the mountains of the Cherokee Forest who have been fatefully thrown to the flatlands of northern cornfields.

J. Cagle

Interview

Gregory Trent settled into his seat and tightened his belt. The big jet bounced once, and he could actually see the massive wing flex with the turbulence. He yawned to pop his ears from the descent preceding the final approach into Nashville, and once again thought to himself how beautiful the city was from above. Percy Priest Lake lay long and blue to the east and the Cumberland was visible just north of town. It was a particularly colorful fall, he noticed, the urban trees in full splendor, and just off the sprawling runway, in the midst of international airway traffic, was a beaver pond, complete with lodge. The plane touched down, and once again he sighed relief at having survived another flight.

After retrieving his baggage and renting a car, he headed northwest. Still early, wisps of fog held tight in the deep hollows, and Gregory was amazed at the quick transition between urban Nashville and "the country." I-24 was attractively billboardless, and it was not long before the smell of dark fired tobacco invaded the car. He lowered the window, allowing the fall scent of Robertson County easier access to his nose. Glancing at the unfolded road map in the seat, he wondered about this Tennessean named Matthew Hills, who had never before granted an interview, despite all the major magazines' efforts. He wondered about the make-up of a man with such a reputation, who shunned attention. Seven entries in Pope and Young and one in Boone and Crockett were hard to keep secret, especially when all were reportedly taken on open lands where trophies are terribly hard to locate, much less harvest. The writer from Atlanta wondered about the Tennessean's secret to success. He also wondered where in the world was a place called Bear Springs which had evidently evaded his map makers.

Passing through Clarksville in route for a town named Dover, he noticed a change: the larger the sections of timber he saw, the older were the vehicles he passed. Country had suddenly turned beautiful backwoods.

A flight of mallards were pitching into a slough off the Cumberland River just before he crossed the bridge into the small town of Dover. There were pick-up trucks mostly, parked along the store fronts as he turned east on Highway 49, and within seconds Gregory had left the entire town behind. He removed the handwritten directions from his pocket and repeatedly glanced from the paper back to the road. Turning south, he followed a series of gravel roads until he was quite sure that he was lost. There were few houses; there was no traffic.

Finally, he saw a white, frame house tucked away in a steep hollow off to his left, and Gregory stopped to ask directions. Gray-white smoke floated thinly from the chimney and a tall man was splitting wood by a shed out back. An old, white faced Lab watched the stranger from the front porch, but after one bark, having completed the job of sounding alarm, she returned to her sleep.

The writer approached the bearded man with the ax. A tear in his jeans exposed white long-johns below the right knee with each swing.

"Howdy," the stranger offered.

The working man glanced up quickly, but continued his swing without a hint of stopping.

"Hello," the man said flatly. "What can I do for you?"

Gregory smiled. "I'm in need of directions. I'm looking for Matthew Hills's place, but my map isn't real good."

The big man stopped briefly to re-position a piece of hickory. "Is Matthew expecting you?"

"Yessir," replied the lost man.

"Let me see your map," said the Tennessean without asking.

Gregory pulled the wrinkled paper from his pocket and presented it across the unsplit piece of firewood. The bearded man stopped, resting his ax against the pile of wood. He studied it briefly and returned it.

"The map's OK," he stated. "Your only problem is that you don't know where you are on the map."

The stranger smiled. "Maybe . . . lost is lost though, and I'm definitely lost."

"Sometimes you think you're lost and you're not and when you try to get unlost, you get really lost. Has that ever happened to you?"

Gregory smiled again, "I'm afraid *you've* lost me. . . ."

The tall man offered his hand. "My name's Matthew Hill. You just think you're lost. You must be Mr. Trent."

Gregory Trent relaxed. "Somehow," he said, "I had you pictured different."

"Why's that?"

"I don't know. Your reputation puts you at about seven feet tall. . . ."

Matthew spit tobacco juice. "Ahh, the truth ain't never disappointing to those lookin' for it. Trouble is, most folks aren't looking for the truth. They're lookin' for a gimmick . . . the spectacular."

"Is that what you're going to give me in our interview, Mr. Hills . . . the truth?"

"Yessir," replied the big man, "and I'm willin' to bet you that when we're through—you won't have a story worth printing, 'cause I ain't got one gimmick or one special secret, and unfortunately, the plain truth don't sell magazines."

They moved to the front porch, Matthew Hills providing fresh coffee as they talked. Gregory Trent produced a small tape recorder.

"Do you mind?" he asked before turning it on.

"Yes, I do," said Matthew politely. "I would prefer that you just take our talk in, and let it roll around, and then you write your piece based on what you feel."

Gregory smiled. "OK, Matthew, but it really makes my job easier. I'm afraid of misquoting you, and the recorder is insurance."

"No," said the Tennessean. "It tempts you into *not* using your own skills as a writer and relying on my quotes. I've read some of your stuff. Let's live dangerously and trust you'll do it right."

The writer paused before continuing. "How come you've been so reluctant to give an interview?"

Matthew rocked the porch swing using the heels of his boots. "The question is why should *I* give an interview on hunting deer? I know several local hunters better than me. . . ."

"Very few people, if anyone, has as many record-book whitetails to their credit as yourself. I think that's ample credentials," offered the stranger.

"Every deer that a hunter seeks out to take is a trophy. That's the real point, I think, not whether they're able to make the books. I regis-tered those deer only for their presence to be documented. Most hunters think older bucks are non-existent."

"Are you saying there are many deer out there that would score in the books?"

"No . . . not at all, but those older deer are there."

"So, how come everybody doesn't find them?"

"Simple," said Matthew, "very few people spend as much time in the woods as I do. If most hunters' priorities were like mine, they would find them too, but they aren't, *and won't be,* 'cause it takes effort to be independently wealthy."

"What do you mean?"

Matthew continued. "Well, it doesn't mean money, that's for sure. But, it does mean that spending your fall in the woods is a high priority—high enough that you change your lifestyle to allow the fall for hunting—everyday. It means, for me, a one acre garden and a small, but ample house, a few cattle to run, and old trucks and working real hard for seven or eight months a year. It means a wife that likes that kind of life, and that pure happiness is hunting close to home."

Gregory paused. "But most people can't do that, Matthew. What advice do you have for those hunters who can't hunt everyday? I'm interested in particulars."

"No, you're wrong. Most people *won't* do what it takes to live out here. They value their security where they are, and I don't fault them for that. It's just very difficult to keep up with what's happening in the woods when spending only the weekends there. Could you keep up with an office job spending two days a week there? No, you couldn't, and it's the same out here. Changes are daily—even in the woods and one will never understand what I'm saying unless enough time is logged *in the woods.* A man can read all the magazines by all the 'so called' experts, and buy all the equipment you all soft sell, but unless he spends a proper amount of time in woods, he is just a well-equipped, well-read, part-time hunter. You show me a hunter who consistently takes record-book bucks and I'll show you a full-time hunter *or* a man rich enough to be escorted into underharvested deer country with a full-time hunter as a guide. It's that simple."

Gregory Trent rocked gently in his chair, squeaking the loose boards on the porch as he moved. "What about equipment? I'm interested in what you shoot."

Matthew smiled. "It's not important what I shoot. It is important that hunters shoot what they hit best with. We all owe it to the animals we hunt to shoot the best equipment we can afford, that offers the best accuracy and reliability. Reliability and consistency are the goals. I don't care whether we're talking a 30-30 or a .270, a compound bow or a long bow. It must shoot to the same place every shot, and it must shoot every time without malfunctions. A hunter must have the common sense to know when accuracy problems are a result of the weapon or himself. If it's the hunter who's wrong, then *he* needs to practice until he's really good. Not good, mind you, *but really good*. We all sinfully lust after many fine guns or bows, but it's important to have *one* that you are totally familiar with."

"Again," asked Gregory, "what do you shoot?"

Matthew paused, almost in resignation. "I shoot a .270, but only because it fits my style of hunting. During bow season, I use a compound bow when I'm in a tree and a recurve when I'm on the ground."

"What about the use of scents," asked the writer. "What do you use?"

"Mostly," Matthew offered, "I don't. I take frequent showers and try to stay clean, but sometimes during bow season I'll use barn yard cow urine. You ever noticed how much it smells like $5.95 deer lure?"

"Have you practiced the use of mock scrapes?"

The Tennessean poured some coffee as he spoke. "A mature buck may make fifty scrapes in one week, and he's a whole lot better at locating 'hot' does than I am. Now why would I waste my time trying to out compete the master doe finder?"

Gregory smiled. "What about the theory of challenging the buck's territory by introducing a 'fake' competitor in order to make him hang around that particular scrape?"

"Is it logical that that old buck is going to waste time trying to find a rival to fight or a girlfriend to breed? Fights occur when rival bucks happen upon each other, mostly in the presence of a 'hot' doe. Sparring occurs from August on between friends. Besides, all the bucks visit each other's scrapes consistently through the season trying to steal the girls' affections. One more 'fake' deer won't cause that much interest."

"Do you call deer?"

"Yes, it's really fun, but certainly nothing new. The Indians did it two hundred years ago, and we just caught on recently to what our forefathers, *who were full-time hunters,* already knew."

A flight of geese passed overhead, giving a natural pause to the interview. The goose calling grew louder, and then faded gradually away to the west. Gregory tapped his pencil against the chair arm.

"What's your message, Mr. Hills? What is it that you would like other hunters to learn from this interview?"

Matthew Hills stopped the swing. "Oh, I guess that we should all be happy with the time we have to spend in the woods, because the land is the real teacher, not magazines. And that all of the really great hunters I've been privileged to know were exceptional woodsmen and proficient shots who practiced the basics religiously and had no gimmicks. Their equipment was accurate and reliable, but not necessarily expensive or exotic. But, more importantly, I think, that if you are a sincere hunter who consistently takes deer, regardless of the size, and your kills are clean, then you are a good hunter, and you should be proud."

Matthew paused again, the chains squeaking as he put the swing in motion.

"So, Mr. Trent, have you got a story?"

Gregory scratched his head. "Honestly?"

"Yep," said the deer hunter.

"I don't think so. Technically you've told me nothing that good hunters don't already know. Most readers are looking for what makes them one up on the next guy. The 'basics' don't sell magazines."

Matthew laughed out loud. "Isn't it funny how a secret can be overlooked because everybody knows it, but hasn't the strength to practice it, because it's so much fun trying to find an easier, quicker way?"

"I don't follow you," said the writer.

"I know," said the Tennessean. "It's like when you think you're lost, and you're not, and when you try to get unlost, suddenly, you're *really* lost.

"What?" asked Gregory.

"Nothing," laughed the hunter. "You keep selling those stories. Some of us backwoods, basic-type guys just love it. . . ."

J. Cagle

The Law

The opossum lay on its side, its right eye mashed against a brown, thumb-nail sized piece of gravel. Its tongue was partially exposed through the death-snarled lips, wedged stiffly between teeth set in hardened jaws. Jesse Barnett stood briefly over the animal, and then moved quickly off the road into the woods on the other side. He thought to himself, as he walked, that no one who knew him would believe he could have such private thoughts, especially about an opossum. It sometimes was bothersome to think that no one really knew him: that he felt tremendous regret in animals being hit by cars. There was absolutely no dignity in road kills, whether it be a hawk or an opossum. Lying blood-crunched on a side road left no memories of past grace or beauty. No living thing deserved a grave of loose gravel and a dented Pabst can for a nearby bone marker. Even an opossum deserved better, he reckoned.

He climbed the ridge, making very little noise in the November leaves. Pausing before entering the openness of the logging road, he crouched at a stump, looking both ways. Once on the rutted trail, Jesse slung the little carbine over his shoulder and walked without a sound. He continued for half a mile until the logging road fell off sharply to a long hollow below.

Jesse Barnett immediately saw the green truck parked below him. He scanned the area for movement, seeking any sign of the driver; but the only movement was a cold rattling of breeze-touched leaves above him. Moving cautiously down the hill, he watched, anticipating the uniformed officer to show himself. At the truck he stopped, almost in mid-stride, like a buck deer testing the wind. He stood stone-like for three minutes.

Brian Harris watched from twenty feet away, his eyes peering through a tangled blowdown of oak branches. He had never seen a man move like Jesse Barnett could move in the woods. The wildlife officer observed that Barnett was ghost-like; he anticipated that any second the vision would whisp away like a woodland mirage. Suddenly, the apparition became very real, its words breaking the silence of the November morning.

"Mr. Harris," the man at the truck began. "You're making me a bit edgy over there behind that blowdown. I just want to talk."

The game warden replied calmly, as if he was not surprised. "Well, I'll tell you, Jesse . . . that carbine makes me a bit edgy myself. How 'bout just laying it over in the back of my truck?"

Barnett studied on that. For a full minute he remained motionless, and then quickly placed the little gun in the truck. He moved to the center of the road and held his arms outstretched.

"There, all clean," he spoke to the blowdown.

Brian Harris emerged from the tangle and walked slowly to the road, facing the bearded woodsman.

"OK, Jesse, what can I do for you?"

"You're bigger than I thought," Jesse replied. "Ain't never seen you up close before."

"What . . . we gonna dance or something? What do you want? You called me . . . remember?"

Jesse Barnett smiled. "You don't like me, do you, Mr. Game Warden?"

Brian Harris shifted his tobacco and spit between them. "Not even a little bit, Jesse."

"Well," Jesse said, "that's too bad, 'cause I ain't never done one thing against you, Mr. Harris. Not in the seven years you've been here have I given you any trouble. You're a good man. I've watched you work. You're fair and tough and people look up to you."

Brian smiled. "You're very good Jesse. I understand a little better now. Not only are you good in the woods; you're a good talker too. It's no wonder all these people make you out so fine. You know, it's a shame. You really could be something, if you would."

"No," Jesse said. "I won't never amount to much, I reckon, least ways in most folk's minds, but I'm trying the best I can. That's all I can do. But I sure do hate it that you hold bad feelings towards me just because you never could catch me wrong."

Brian Harris smiled before he spit again. "You're the best I've ever seen, Jesse, but that doesn't mean you're uncatchable. I'm in no hurry."

"Did you ever figure that maybe you never caught me because maybe all them stories you've heard was wrong? Maybe there's nothing to catch me for," Jesse offered.

"Yeah," Brian replied, "and maybe I'll just flap my arms and fly back to town, but I kinda doubt it."

Jesse Barnett laughed for the first time, and it echoed off the ridge behind the wildlife officer. There was an uncomfortable silence afterwards, both men looking the other straight on.

"I need a favor," said Jesse. "Problem is that you owe me nothing."

"That's right," replied the man in uniform.

"So, I'm gonna show you my good faith before I ask. I promise you that no one who kills a deer wrong in my section of the county will go unpunished, and that for three years you will have no serious poaching down here."

Brian Harris raised an eyebrow. "And you can just say it and it becomes law, is that right?"

"Yessir," he said quickly.

"Well, if I'm the great game warden you just told me I am, then how come I haven't been able to stop it . . . and you can just snap your fingers and it's done?"

"That's simple," replied Jesse. "You've got rules in your law. That's what makes you an honorable man. You've got rules. . . . I'm just an old red-necked country boy, and I ain't got no rules. That's my law."

Brian Harris walked to the truck and retrieved the carbine from the back. He popped the clip and ejected a shell from the chamber, catching it in the air before it hit the ground.

"I don't make deals," he said, tossing the little gun to its owner. "You show me your good intentions . . . we'll talk again." Brian laid the clip on a stump by the truck.

"Fair enough," Jesse said.

The wildlife officer climbed in his truck and started the engine.

"Hey!"

Brian rolled down the window and looked at the man in the road.

"For the record, I never offered you a deal . . . just made a promise."

The officer smiled. "I'm trying to figure out how much a promise is worth from a man who doesn't have rules."

Jesse Barnett tipped his hat farther forward on his head.

"I reckon you'll find out, Mr. Harris. . . ."

Two days later, Brian Harris pulled into the graveled parking lot of Ted's Market. He climbed the worn concrete steps and was just before entering the country store when a truck pulled up.

"Hey? Mr. Harris . . . ," came the call from the old truck. "Can we see you a minute?"

Brian recognized the pair and turned, taking a seat on the knife-scarred wooden bench. The two men climbed the steps and stopped, looking down between their feet.

"Hello Snookie . . . Pete, what's going on?" asked Brian.

"Well," started Snookie as he puffed on his Camel. "Me and Pete, well, we got drunk a week ago Friday night and killed us a doe deer. And we've felt plum bad about it, killin' it at night and all, and well, we've decided to throw ourselves at the mercy of the court."

The game warden smiled. "Since when did killin' deer at night make you feel bad, Snookie. I've caught you three times in seven years. It's cost you one old truck and three worthless rifles. You suddenly got religious or something?"

Pete almost laughed. "Yeah . . . that's it. Sort of."

"Well, I'll tell you boys," Brian said. "You've had your fun this morning. I've got work to do. Ya'll will excuse me." The wildlife officer stood up and turned toward the store's door.

Pete Bowry jumped in front of the officer.

"You've got to believe us, Mr. Harris. We're guilty. We've got the deer in the back of the truck there. C'mon . . . we're serious. You've *got* to arrest us."

At the truck, Brian inspected the doe deer and then rubbed his head.

"You know, Snookie, that I can seize this truck," he whispered.

"Yessir," Snookie replied. "That would be good. I deserve it. I've really been a no-good snake-in-the-grass all these years, as far as the game populations go, but we're a turnin' over new leaves."

"What'd he threaten you with?" the officer asked.

"What?" asked Snookie.

"Don't 'what' me," Brian blurted. "I want to know what Jesse Barnett did to make you turn yourself in. He did talk to you, didn't he?"

Snookie didn't hesitate. "Yessir, he sure did, and he said you'd be asking about him," Snookie paused.

"Well?" Brian said.

"Well what?" asked Snookie.

"How did he get you to do this?"

"Oh," Pete interrupted. "He just said that he'd consider it a personal favor if we went straight."

"That's all?"

"Yessir . . . ol' Jesse . . . he's a fine feller. Did we ever tell you about the time he shot that buck at 250 yards with that little carbine he carries? Right in the neck . . . he sure can shoot. . . ."

"Shut up," Brian Harris said flatly.

"Yessir," Pete responded.

In the next eleven days, nine individuals turned themselves into Brian Harris for various big game violations. Some were more hesitant than others, but all were intent on reform. At the end of the twelfth day, the officer drove a secluded gravel road to Barnett's house. He turned on a one-lane creek-graveled path that led through a mature oak stand along the creek. Brian was surprised that the house looked so neat in the distance. He wondered if the man was married or had children. It was not really fair that his entire opinion of the man had been based upon stories. He stopped the truck at the front porch and got out, listening for any signs of life.

The front door opened slowly, and Jesse Barnett emerged wearing blue jeans and a flannel shirt. He sat on the front steps before speaking.

"Hello, Mr. Harris," he offered. "Have you had supper? I'm frying up some quail if you're hungry."

"No thanks, I won't be long. Just figured we needed to talk."

"Well," Jesse smiled. "Have you seen a change in the community's concern for wildlife conservation?"

Brian moved to the porch side of the truck and leaned against the front fender, crossing his arms.

"Yeah," he said. "It's amazing and I can't even get one person to admit you threatened him!"

"That's cause I didn't," Jesse said. "These are good people down here, Mr. Harris. They listen to reason. They're a bit rough around the edges, but they see clear enough."

"And what did you make them see?" asked Brian.

A beagle rounded the corner of the house and playfully attacked its owner on the steps. Jesse rubbed its ears.

"Oh, that we need your help on something, and the only way to get your help is to prove we care."

"What kind of help?"

"We want to stop something," Jesse continued. "Have you heard about the plan to put one of them toxic waste places in this county?"

Brian nodded. "Yes, but I don't think anything is definite."

"Well, I happen to know that old man Diggon has offered to sell 'em his place. And that's just right over that ridge."

Brian Harris tried to be positive. "Shoot . . . they'll have to have public hearings and studies before they decide. Chances are that they'll find someplace else."

Jesse patted the dog's head and looked up. "And who cares about this land down here? Nobody except us poor country folk that live here. I'm not real smart, but I know that if you want to find an out-of-the-way place to put poison, that this is the place. And politics . . . boy, I'll tell ya. Everybody should really fear our politics. We actually swung getting electricity down here last year."

"I'll tell you how bad it is," Jesse continued. "It's so bad that the highest public official we know to go to for help is the county game warden. . . ."

The game warden laughed out loud. "You're in *real* trouble."

Suddenly, after the laughter died, the man on the porch was very serious. He gently pushed the dog down to the ground.

"We ain't got much, Mr. Harris. These hills and trees and creeks are about all. And we know that if you have that . . . that stuff close . . . that everything is poisoned. Everything dies . . . but more than anything, *more than anything*. . . . I don't want to kill anybody. I will not allow them to put that stuff here, Mr. Harris. I will fight them. It's the only way we know, . . . and that's why we need your help. If you help us stop this thing, then maybe we won't have to kill people, or get killed, or go to jail."

Brian Harris walked closer to the man on the steps and put out his hand.

"I give you my word . . . I'll try."

And the two shook hands. "We appreciate it, Mr. Harris. We know you're a good man. If you try, we'll be obliged . . . you know, life's really crazy. In 1967 I was eighteen. I was ten thousand miles from here killing people who never did one thing against me. They never threatened my home with poison . . . life sure is funny, don't you think, Mr. Harris?"

Brian Harris smiled. "Sometimes, Mr. Barnett, it just takes us awhile to understand. . . ."

Jesse Barnett looked up and Brian noticed a saddened strain in the woodsman's eyes. He started to talk, but stopped, and then after a second, continued.

"I remember being so confused. I was very good at what I did. . . . I guess being raised in the Tennessee woods is good training for fighting in jungles and such. But there was no dignity in it and, really, there needs to be dignity in death, no matter what it is that dies. And I just can't see no dignity at all in slowly dying from someone else's poison. It ain't right. It just ain't right."

A chilling wind found the back of Brian Harris's neck, causing him to shiver.

"I would like to have some dignity in my death, Mr. Harris."

Four miles to the east, an opossum walked lazily into the center of the county road. He sniffed at a Marlboro butt and looked up to see two lights that burned his brain. He thought about running, but got confused. He simply shut his eyes to avoid the light and waited for the danger to go away.

Goodmornin' and Amen

Alan Pearson moved the boat into the main channel of the river and opened the throttle on the Mercury. The January air was painful, the cold tearing at his face, forcing his eyes to water. It was a short run to the mouth of the next creek, but the gloved hand on the throttle control was quickly numbed from the wind. The waves slammed against the bow of the boat, occasionally spraying him with a frigid mist. He did not like the river in winter, but he longed to catch sauger. One went with the other.

He had learned to enjoy Mondays, his least busy day of the week. It seemed few people took Mondays off from work, leaving fishing waters relatively uncrowded. Alan Pearson enjoyed solitude, perhaps the best part of fishing, so he fished on Mondays when most folks returned to the crowds.

He saw the boat drifting across the mouth of the creek and was somewhat surprised that another fisherman had found his spot. On the other hand, maybe it was he who was intruding, Alan considered. He throttled down, keeping a respectful distance, and killed the engine. The aluminum boat was still slapped by the waves as he quickly baited up and tossed the line over. Lowering the minnowed jig twenty feet he felt for the drop off and began bumping the bottom. He had only drifted fifteen feet when the first fish hit. He set the hook, feeling the immediate resistance. On the ultralight rig the fight was respectful and he took his time, never rushing the fish until it broke water at the boat. With his right hand he lifted the yellow-brown fish into the boat, carefully removing the hook from its toothed mouth. He studied the primitive looking fish before chunking it into the live well. The sweetest meat swimming, he thought. Fourteen more to go.

Alan looked up to check his position. To his surprise, he had drifted further than expected during the landing of the fish. He could see the other fisherman watching him across the fifty yards of open water. Alan waved. The fisherman raised his hand in a friendly response. Their boats drifted closer and closer as Alan rebaited the jig.

"Goodmornin'," the other fisherman yelled.

"Mornin'," Alan replied. "Doing any good?"

The older fisherman sculled his boat closer until the bows were almost touching. He used his paddle to keep the boats apart.

"I reckon I'm finished," he continued. "Fifteen's all they allow. I've had good luck drifting both sides of the drop off."

"Appreciate it," Alan smiled. "Any size?"

"Yeah, they're all good fish," he answered. "I haven't seen you out here before. I'm Lee Tuttle. If you fish these parts much, I reckon we'll cross paths again."

"Alan Pearson. Pleased to meet you, Lee."

He started to shake hands, but then thought better of it, considering the dipping boats and slapping waves.

"You're the new preacher, aren't you?" Lee asked.

Alan quickly studied the man. The insulated coveralls made him look heavy. His face was round and weathered.

"Yes, I am. Been here about six months, I guess," Alan replied. "Have we met before?"

"No. It's a small town. Word gets around."

Alan tossed his jig over the side and let out line.

"Don't mind if I fish while we drift, do you?"

"Not at all. I like a preacher who fishes. Shows me something," Lee said.

Alan smiled. "What's that, Mr. Tuttle. What's it show you?"

Lee took his bow line and tied it off to the preacher's boat and then scooted to the middle seat, holding the boats together with his hand.

"A deeper understanding, maybe," Lee said. "You have a family?"

"Wife and two children. Boy and a girl."

Alan worked the rod with his left hand from the front of the boat. He noticed Lee's hand. It was big with small white scars that interrupted the winter tan.

"You?" Alan asked.

"Kids are grown and gone. My wife passed away two years ago. Just me," he said a bit uncomfortably.

"You farm?" asked the preacher.

"Farm and fish," he nodded.

The sauger hit the jig on the downfall. Alan barely felt the tap, tried to set the hook, and missed.

"How 'bout church?" he continued. "I like church members who fish."

Lee smiled. "Is that an invitation?"

"Absolutely. Where's your church?"

"Lots of places, depending on the season," Lee said.

Alan looked puzzled. "What church, I mean."

"No church," Lee shook his head.

The boats rocked in the waves. A flight of mallards worked the open water in plain view and touched the surface in nine separate splashes.

"Well, I don't know where you attend, but I wish you'd come visit me, one fisherman to another," Alan tried sincerely.

Lee looked across the boat at the preacher, purposefully studying the young man.

"I'll tell you, son. You come to church with me Sunday morning. Then I'll go with you."

"I'm pretty busy on Sunday, you understand. I don't think that would work," Alan smiled.

"It'll work," Lee said. "My service is real early."

Alan set the hook, working the fish slowly to the surface. He needed the time to think, wondering about the invitation.

"How's he feel?" Lee asked.

"Good. He's a good fish."

"Well, how about Sunday?"

"I don't know," Alan said, lifting the two pound sauger into the boat.

"Nice fish," Lee smiled. "You take care of yourself, Mr. Pearson."

Lee untied the bowline and pushed off, separating the boats. It was a quick separation, throwing the preacher a bit off guard. The old fisherman moved to the motor.

"What time's the service?" Alan asked suddenly.

Lee looked around. "Sunrise."

"Where?"

"I'll pick you up, hour before sunrise."

"You know where I live?"

"No. But I'll find you. Deal?"

Alan paused. A fish hit the jig, jerking his arm.

"Deal." And the fish fought hard as Lee Tuttle's boat disappeared in the distance.

In the six days that followed, Alan had asked several people about the fisherman named Lee Tuttle. All had known him. All had given similar responses. Hard worker. Good man. Keeps to himself after the death of his wife. One had said, "Tougher'n boot leather." Another replied, "I wouldn't want to fight him." None had said anything about his spiritual strength or mentioned church affiliations.

Rising early on Sunday morning was nothing new to Alan Pearson. He had often reviewed his sermon in the pre-light hours. The house was quiet. The world was asleep except for farmers and fishermen, he thought. Headlights from the truck flashed across the wall, and he exited the house through the garage, closing the door quietly behind him. Alan approached the truck, noticing a cold fog was falling. The night was black. No moon. No stars. He opened the passenger door and looked in.

"Mornin'," Lee smiled. "You're overdressed, Preacher. Grab some boots. I've got you an extra set of coveralls."

Alan returned to the garage where he retrieved a pair of Brownings and walked back to the truck. The warmth inside the truck felt good.

"I didn't know how to dress," he said.

Lee put the truck in reverse and backed out of the driveway. He went through all the gears before talking again.

"When you're with me, NEVER dress up, Mr. Pearson. It's a rule I've lived with my entire adult life. There's soap-clean and work-dirty. That's all."

They drove through town and continued west, taking a dirt road that curved and forked and curved and forked some more. The truck forded a small creek and Alan thought the water might come inside the cab. They tried to talk, but it was not comfortable, so they stopped trying. Lee turned onto a logging road and put the truck in four-wheel drive continuing deeper into the woods. The road was rutted badly and a couple of times the preacher thought they were stuck, but Lee seemed unconcerned. They stopped when the road ended at a fallen white oak.

"Where are we?" Alan asked.

"Church," Lee stated flatly as he quietly shut the door behind him. They moved to the back of the truck where Lee removed two pairs of coveralls from the camper top. Suiting up, they then moved through the woods behind the white oak, following a faint trail disclosed by Lee's flashlight.

They walked for thirty minutes, gradually climbing higher, and passed a sign nailed to a tree. National Wildlife Refuge. Finally Lee stopped. The bluff ended abruptly and in the dawn's first light, Alan could see a blackened river bottom below him. The river extended on either side of them, a winding black ribbon. Flat fields lay beyond the river for at least a mile, and Alan could see flooded areas throughout the fields.

"See those two cedars, the ones slanting out over the bluff?" Lee whispered.

"Yeah."

"Are you afraid of heights?" he asked.

"Yes," Alan nodded.

"That's why I brought the ropes," he smiled. "So am I."

Alan followed Lee to the cedars and watched him tie the rope to a large hickory. Two ends were left long enough to reach the edge of the bluff.

"What are you doing?" Alan asked.

"Here, tie this end around your waist. It'll help take the jitters away," Lee said.

"What jitters? What are you doing?" the preacher asked again.

"We're going to straddle those cedars. The ones slanting over the bluff, unless you don't want to use the rope."

"Do what! That's a two hundred foot drop off! Look, Mr. Tuttle. I don't understand," Alan said.

"I know. Trust me. You'll understand in a minute."

"Do you take all the preachers you like up here?" Alan asked.

"Nope," he said, tying the rope around his waist. "You're the first to take me up on my offer."

Alan began tying the rope. "I'm crazy," he whispered. Lee sat on the ground at the edge of the bluff, straddling the trunk of the leaning cedar. Scooting forward, his feet went over the edge, dangling in the air, his backside sitting on the tree.

"Like this," he whispered.

"I like it right here. Whatever you've got in mind has got to be just as good back here," the preacher said.

"No," Lee said. "It's better out here. You'll see!"

The preacher sat, inching forward toward the edge. His boots left the ground, extending into the air over the river below. He placed his hands on the smooth bark of the cedar and pulled. The tree appeared firmly rooted in the bluff earth, so he went further until he sat on the trunk. It was surprisingly comfortable, if he didn't look down. He looked at Lee, who was smiling back at him.

"Good," Lee whispered. "Now, we pray."

"No problem," Alan Pearson said. "Just tell me, Mr. Tuttle. Are you sane?"

"Just pray. You'll see."

So Alan prayed, with his eyes wide open looking over the expansive river bottom before him. As the light grew, he noticed the land below was dotted with thousands of moving black specks. Extended beyond the safety of the ground behind him, he almost could feel like he was hovering in open air. It was then, when the light became good enough to see in the grayness, that he heard the geese, the moving dots below him.

It was if they were waiting for some mystery leader to instruct them because when the first goose called, the others followed until the entire flock was in a chorus, a maddening, harmonic, concerto of nature's orchestra that made the preacher's heart beat faster and his shoulders tremble. He watched from his perch as the birds took to the air, like a feathered ocean wave in a hurricane of living power. The goose calling grew even louder, echoing off the bluff below them as the birds came closer, rising in a beating cloud of honks and wings and flying life that overwhelmed the two men on the trees. The power of the flock's movement drove Alan Pearson to hold the tree, like when he was a child embracing his father after being frightened. The geese, maybe twenty thousand in the ascending flock, rose from fields below to clear the height of the bluff. They only missed the cedars by a few feet in their flight from the river, encircling the two men as the birds departed. Alan felt as if he were in the flock, flying with them, the thousands of calling birds all around him, the air from their wings moving his hair, and he was suddenly crying. It was a cry he had never before experienced, borne of pure awe. Pure flight. Pure elevation.

And they were gone. The last calling birds somewhere behind

him were silent. He looked at Lee Tuttle, who was hugging his own tree, feeling his own thoughts. They were suddenly just two winter fishermen who had crossed paths on the river.

"She made me promise that I would worship every Sunday," he whispered from his tree. "I have kept my word in my own way," he said. "Do you think she understands, Preacher?"

"I think, Mr. Tuttle, that you are perhaps the sanest man I've ever known. I think she's very proud."

Alan Pearson began the eleven o'clock service with a peacefulness that would have been hard for him to explain. He had not seen Lee Tuttle's face in the congregation when he surveyed the crowd, but it did not bother him. For some reason, he did not expect the fisherman to be present. It was during the silent meditation, just prior to the prayer, that he heard the back door of the church open. Actually, it wasn't the door he heard, but the outside sounds the opened door let in. It was the call of a cardinal, a redbird in the church yard, he figured. Somehow the bird call signaled the faint sound of a goose call memory, and he smiled to himself. He began the prayer, hearing his words echo off the church walls, wishing they could have the power of voices off the bluff he had heard earlier that morning. He paused before ending the prayer.

". . . and Father we pray that each of us will reach out in our own way to those who would listen, and be brave, so that the miracle of your hands will surround us, and give us strength. Amen."

The preacher opened his eyes to see Lee Tuttle sitting in the back pew. He wore no tie nor expensive shoes, but he looked real clean. And he was smiling. Alan Pearson smiled back because he really liked fishermen in his congregation. Like winter and sauger fishing, one went with the other.

The Guide

The osprey perched statue-like on the snag above the creek. The brilliant white of its belly contrasted sharply to the darkness of the wings, and even from far away, Dirk Carpenter could see the bloody fish meat it held securely within its talons. He lowered the binoculars, studying the blue-green ribbon of creeks that snaked below him before emptying into the isolated cove off the Tennessee River. The early summer sunrise had chilled the air, and he shivered slightly before turning toward the house. The house wasn't much, he reckoned, as he noticed the porch was in need of repair, but the view was really nice. This far back, there was no traffic noise to poison the natural sounds. Dirk was only seventeen, but had matured enough to hate the sound of traffic.

Pete Carpenter repositioned a rod in the boat, and then watched as his son approached. The boy was already darkly tanned and his short-cropped hair was bleached from his hatred of hats, allowing the sun's rays to alter the color. Although still in high school, Pete Carpenter's son was considered the premier guide for this section of the river, the father reckoned. It was a nice thought. There was no grown man who knew this land and its waters better than Dirk Carpenter, his son, and the boy's reputation was fully grown . . . far exceeding his actual years. Pete checked the trailer's tightness on the truck bumper's ball with a quick jerk, and then limped toward the passenger door, his artificial leg squeaking with each step.

"You drive," he instructed his son. "You're the guide. . . ."

"I'm not guiding you," smiled Dirk. "You were *my* guide . . . remember . . . and besides, you're not a paying customer. You know what that means . . . ?"

"Yeah . . . ," said Pete. "It means I'll help clean the fish, but don't push your luck, boy. Your Mom and I made you . . . we can make another one just like you, if need be."

Dirk laughed. "Yessir, Pop, you just keep on dreamin'. . . ."

And the morning was suddenly invaded by tires on grinding gravel. In the distance, they saw a Blazer pulling a bright, sparkling blue bass boat.

"I thought you were gonna take the day off," asked the father.

"I am . . . ," Dirk replied. "Bad timing . . . in another three minutes we would have missed 'em."

The strangers stopped at the Carpenter house. Two men, both wearing new caps, stepped out. The driver, while attempting to read a note from his pocket, spoke first.

"We're looking for a Dirk Carpenter."

Dirk leaned against the truck door.

"What for?" he asked.

"We need a guide for one day. Man in town said you were the best . . . we want the best."

"Who said I was him?" Dirk asked.

"Well, are you?" asked the other stranger.

"Where *are* you from?" asked the guide.

"New Jersey," answered the driver.

"Oh . . . I see, well, I *am* him, but I can't help you today, 'cause I'm takin' my dad fishing. Already promised. Sorry."

"You don't understand," said the driver. "I need your services, and I'll pay for them. You are a business man, aren't you?"

"No sir," Dirk said, "*you* don't understand. I'm a fisherman. . . ."

"I'll pay two-hundred dollars and we use my boat and gas. All you do is point us in the right direction."

Pete Carpenter repositioned his cap on his head, and spoke slowly, but deliberately.

"Son, can I see you a second . . . on this side of the truck. Excuse me, gentlemen, but we need a conference here."

Dirk rounded the front of the truck as the two from New Jersey regrouped at the bass boat. Both pairs whispered.

"Son, this man's got more money than sense . . . take the boys fishin'."

"But Dad, we've planned this day for a month. I'm booked solid for the next three weeks and we'll not have another. . . ."

"Get the money up front and take the boys fishin' . . . you and I'll have time to catch up. They don't offer scholarships to UT for fishin' . . . you'll need the money."

Ernie Pienelli smiled to his partner. "That's more money than the kid's seen in a year. He'll go. Look at that house and truck. Two hundred dollars would buy anything down here . . . anything."

Dirk's Dad turned from the truck and limped toward the house. "Have a good day, son." Dirk grabbed a pack from the Alumnacraft and threw it in the sparkling blue bass boat.

"You just bought yourself a guide for the day. I'll need the money in advance. . . ."

Dirk sat at the bow, operating the trolling motor; he did not fish, and only spoke when directing their casting efforts toward unseen, underwater structures that usually held fish. It was a matter of principle with him. They paid him two hundred dollars; they should get two hundred dollars worth of guidance. And, from the first stop, they caught fish. It was peculiar, he thought, how different the clients could be. There were those who he automatically liked, but refrained from joining in conversations with, for fear of interrupting *their* day. In his mind, the guide should always be pleasant, answer general questions, but more importantly, act like an intuition for their efforts, and allow friends to carry on their friendship without the strained presence of a stranger. And then there were clients like these: boisterous, rich, egocentric, and generally inept at matching their skills with wildlife more intelligent than retarded 'possums.

At eleven minutes after ten, Ernie Pienelli felt a tap. Dirk saw the tap in the fisherman's slack line and saw it slowly moving off. . . .

"Hit him . . . hard," Dirk suggested. "That's a good fish."

"Oh yeah," Ernie excitedly answered. "I just want you to show me where they are. I don't need your advice on how to catch them. I was landing hunker bass on a worm when you were in diapers . . . ," Ernie released the spool, allowing the fish to move. "I'll hit him when I'm good and ready."

Dirk smiled. "Suits me . . . I didn't realize you like tryin' to land good fish that have wrapped themselves around forty hang-ups. He's headin' out of the clear into some thick stuff, but you go ahead . . . I'm only a kid and all."

Ernie hit the fish, and the fight lasted just long enough for the fisherman from New Jersey to understand *it was a really good bass,* and the kid was right. The seventeen pound line snapped after four seconds. Ernie threw the rod against the bottom of the boat and entered into a series of cussing that echoed off the timbered ridges above them.

"Why didn't you tell me!" he yelled at the young guide.

Dirk Carpenter did not look at the red-faced man standing in the middle of the boat, but activated the trolling motor, moving the boat forward, toward a small inlet off the main creek channel.

The angry man yelled. "Stop the boat, and get me a beer. I paid you and you're going to earn it!"

The young Tennessean never acknowledged the yells. He looked straight ahead, guiding the boat toward a shallow bar that extended between two deep channels. "You better back off, Ernie," he whispered. "Cool down . . . before you blow a gasket."

Ernie started toward the bow when the fisherman in the stern yelled.

"Look, Ernie! What a fish."

Forty degrees off the starboard side, against the sand bar was a spawning largemouth. Its dorsal and tail fins were visible above the water, and the bass was enormous.

"How much will she weigh, Ernie?" asked his companion.

Ernie removed his hat. "She'll break ten pounds if she's an ounce," he marveled. "What about it—country boy? What will it weigh?"

Dirk paused. "Doesn't make any difference what it weighs, and by the way, I'll bet it's male, you won't get it to hit anything. It's not interested in eating right now. Leave it alone."

"Yeah, sure . . . the trophy fish of a lifetime and you casually say 'leave it alone.'" Ernie mocked. All the time, the man from New Jersey was rummaging through his tackle box, until finally he emerged with an extremely large treble hook.

"She won't have to be hungry with this baby," he laughed and immediately began tying on the large hook. The smaller man at the motor was laughing.

"This is going to be great," he yelled. "Go get him, Ernie."

Dirk Carpenter ran his hand across his eyes and then through his hair.

"Hey . . . ," the guide said, but the two were not listening.

"Hey!" he repeated.

"What . . . ?" returned Ernie angrily.

"You are not going to snag that fish. It ain't fair."

"You want to bet . . . just watch!" And Ernie stood, testing the weight of the heavy hooks.

The young Tennessean turned the boat into deeper water; the hum of the trolling motor was muffled by the lapping water against the side of the boat.

"Stop!" yelled the large man. "Right now, boy! You're fired!"

"OK," Dirk said, "That makes it easier. Take me to the bank then, seeing as I'm fired."

"Afterwards," Ernie said. "Right now, you just sit down and shut up."

"You are not going to snag that fish," said the guide flatly.

Ernie turned back toward the sand bar and started the cast toward the fish, as Dirk Carpenter reached into his pack. In one fluid motion, the young Tennessean pulled a Smith and Wesson nine-millimeter automatic from a holster, flicked off the safety, opened a storage compartment under his seat exposing the naked hull, and fired three rounds into the bottom of the twenty thousand dollar, sparkling blue bass boat from New Jersey.

Ernie Pienelli stood awestruck, staring at the young man with the pistol. The smaller fisherman, attempting to hide from the boy, was hugging the two-hundred-horsepower Evinrude.

"Now, that I have your attention," Dirk continued, "I'll repeat myself once more . . . *take me to the bank*, which would be a good idea anyway, considering we're sittin' in about twenty feet of water and after every five seconds, I'm going to shoot another hole in the bottom of this really nice boat."

And he fired once more, the spent brass bouncing across a portion of fiberglass deck. Ernie was suddenly interested in starting the Evinrude, and within seconds the boat was beached on the opposite bank.

Dirk grabbed his pack and stepped to the bank, the pistol still in his hands.

"If you get the bow far enough up the bank, you'll be able to bilge pump out the water, and then if you really go fast, you should be able to make it back to the ramp. It's only about a mile downstream . . . but, remember this, *you should go home,* because in Tennessee there is a respect for these animals that you don't have. It is an honorable thing to be a woodsman in this state—and you boys, well . . . you don't cut it. Go home, and take your lousy two hundred dollars with you."

He threw the two bills from his pocket, and they landed in the water at the boats side. The young guide backed away until, in a thicket of honeysuckle he turned, starting his five mile hike over land toward home. It was really peculiar how people's priorities get confused, he reckoned. And in his mind, there was extreme pity for those less fortunate than himself: those poor individuals who drive sparkling bass boats instead of old Alumnacrafts, and watch graphically enhanced depth recorders instead of morning-feeding ospreys.

He glanced at his watch as he crested the top of the ridge. By the time he got home there would still be time for him and his father to get in a full half day in the Alumnacraft. A good fishing partner is especially hard to find, which makes it especially precious when he is your father, squeaky leg and all.

Summer

Gathering together in Tennessee during the summer, there were almost a hundred of them, ranging in age from a few months to ninety. They rented Group Camp Number One at Montgomery Bell State Park, and it cost them seven hundred dollars for one week. The accommodations were less than modern. Paper towels were poked in holes in the screen windows of the cabins to keep the bugs out at night. Mice shared their quarters along with flying squirrels. Raccoons walked their porches after the sun went down. Everyone shared community bathrooms, having to pro-

claim their presence upon entering to insure privacy. The bathroom rock walls grew a healthy crop of green moss, and the floors stayed perpetually wet from leaky shower stalls. At meal times, they cooked their own food. The place was worth seven hundred bucks, however, and a lot more.

They converged from the south mostly, Texas, Georgia, Virginia, and Tennessee. Some came from as far away as Nebraska. They were all Tennesseans through their blood, and the majority came from towns like Tennessee Ridge, Erin, Clarksville, Jackson, and Nashville. The focal point of their ancestry, however, was Houston County, the geographical location that had originally dispersed them and still was home to the family patriarchs, those oldest of the family whose presence brought their children and grandchildren and great-grandchildren home to reunite, a family reunion. A Roby Reunion.

At forty-one, G.W. had been to family reunions before, his entire life taking part in other reunion activities. Basically, those were one day affairs where the kids were thrown together with distant cousins they never had time to really know. Adults visited quickly with relatives almost forgotten and skimmed the surface of time elapsed. Not unlike high school reunions, forced and difficult, they were unreal attempts at covering the aging process.

Sitting under the large maple where the outside cooking took place just down the hill from the horseshoe pits, he wondered why the Roby reunion was different. He tried to sort it out. He had time. There was no hurry. Nothing was scheduled for him to absolutely have to do for the next four days. This reunion allowed time to sort things out, time to ponder things that normally would not have a priority in his thinking process. Karen and Kristen walked across the grass in front of him toward the large dining hall. They looked like friends. He liked that and smiled, lifting his tea glass toward them as their eyes met.

"Where you going?" he yelled.

"Softball game on the hill," his wife yelled back.

"C'mon!" waved his daughter.

"I'm cookin' the hog. I'm comfortable."

They waved at him and disappeared around the hill as a clanging of steel set off a cheer from the horseshoe pits. Ronnie apparently had found his distance and spin, much to the dismay of his opponent. The lawn chair spectators joined in the bantering, remembering that when Ronnie found his mark, it was as if his horse shoes were smart bombs carrying their own sophisticated guidance systems. Don, his competition, protested the ringer, recommending that Ronnie be handicapped like in trap shoots where the player is forced to shoot from a farther distance, preferably, Don motioned, from the cooking tree, some fifty yards away.

Hearing the argument, G.W. smiled, lifting the top to the cooker. The smoke immediately attacked his eyes, causing brief pain and tears. The whole hog was no longer pink, but was taking on a smoky, brown color. He doused the hog with the old family recipe. It rolled off the meat and sizzled on the coals, leaving a brown residue of secret spices on the skin. The aroma drifted downwind, prompting a minor migration of Robys to the cooker along with their lawn chairs and tea glasses. They set up a new circle, occupying the slowly moving shade provided by the cooking tree. Wayne crossed his legs, then quickly uncrossed them, leaned forward in the chair, adding an emphasis to his words. He spoke with his right hand, as well as his words.

"I tell ya, babe, the hog looks fine. Now, some of the old timers are gonna give you their ideas of how you could do it this way or that, and so forth and so on, but you just hang in there, babe. You're doin' fine."

"Old timers," Bitsy interrupted. "How old are you, Wayne?"

"You don't worry about that, Bit," Wayne argued with his cousin. "You just worry about the money end of the deal. You and Maida are the bankers in this crowd. Leave the serious cooking to us."

"See there," she motioned with her glass. She turned back to G.W. "Listen to Wayne's advice and don't listen to him."

"Now, Bitsy, all I was getting around to is I think G.W.'s got the fire a tad too hot, and he's gonna burn the danged pig up, but that's all right, cause we're all in this together."

Laughter erupted under the cooking tree just as a crack of the bat turned their attention to the hill. Loud cheering followed the runner from base to base.

"Where's Edwin and Sue?" someone asked.

"Umping the softball game," came a reply.

G.W. watched the vein in his left foot just below his ankle, extending into the tennis shoe. It beat with his heart, clearly visible in its work, coursing family blood through his body. Family blood. It had started a long time ago.

The family had traced themselves back to Barton Roby of North Carolina in 1799. Greenbriar Wilson Roby, one of Barton's sons, moved to Georgia, married Mary Elizabeth Freeman, took out for Missouri, Kentucky, and finally settled in Stewart, Tennessee, where their first son, Zephaniah, was born in 1869. Zeph grew up a Tennessean and became a telegraph operator for the L. and N. Railroad.

In 1855, a German carpenter and cabinet maker stowed away on a steamer to become an American. He started out in Beaver Falls, Pennsylvania, but by 1870 had established a home place in Stewart County, Tennessee. He bought 128 acres of good Tennessee ground, and in 1873 George and his wife, Sophia Miller, had a daughter named Sallie Ann.

Zephaniah Roby married Sallie Ann in June of 1892, and was appointed Postmaster, serving three consecutive terms. In 1915, he tried the mercantile trade, liked it, and stayed in that business for thirty-nine years. He also farmed and operated the largest dairy business in the county. Sallie Ann and Zeph Roby were happily married for fifty-two years.

Descendants of their nine children were scattered all around him. G.W. watched as they talked and laughed, mixing their ankle blood in family words.

He heard the sound of the electric wheelchair before looking up. It was a smooth, humming, winding-of-gears noise that moved over the grass like a breeze. He watched as Edwin approached with Sue, his wife, along side. It was hard to visualize his cousin in the chair, a vivid contrast to his pre-accident memory.

Edwin was a large man, six-foot-five or six, and weighed about two hundred and fifty pounds. G.W. remembered changing a tire on a Ford Mustang while his older cousin had picked up the rear end. The jack had been lost, and Edwin scolded him the entire time while holding the vehicle off the ground. There had been no strain in his voice, G.W. remembered. He watched the chair grow nearer, finally realizing that the big man's strength was not muscular. It was something much deeper. Edwin purposefully bumped his lawn chair with the motorized wheelchair.

"Want to arm wrestle?" he asked smiling.

"Absolutely not," G.W. replied. "The memory of your arms could beat me."

They were suddenly overwhelmed by little people, boys to be exact, with sloshy-wet tennis shoes, scratched arms, worm-dirty fingernails, poison-ivied hands, and big eyes. They converged on the mechanical chair, grabbing wheels, controls, legs, and arms. The chair sped forward, backwards, and did a quick circle running over all in its path. Kids scattered, fell, and came limping back to regain their original enthusiasm.

"Man, that thing's awesome," one said rubbing his leg.

Edwin was laughing. "Y'all OK?"

"Look, grandaddy! Look what Jared caught!"

Jared held up a small bass, now deceased by an accident with a wheelchair.

Edwin whistled. "That's a fine one. How come y'all didn't save him for the tournament tomorrow?"

"We're practicin'," Chad added. "Pre-tournament scouting."

"You better practice washing up before supper. . . ."

There was a scream from the dining hall. It sounded painful. Adults with small children started counting heads, wondering if the cry belonged to them. Quickly, a mother was visible on the hill, turned toward the cooking tree and yelled.

"Don't worry! It's mine. Nothing but multiple wasp stings!" Penny was used to emergencies. With triplets, she carried a first aid kit wherever she went in anticipation of disaster.

A breeze blew through the cooking tree, easing the August stickiness. It moved the maple leaves above them and carried the smoke from the hog sideways across the ground.

"Gonna rain," Edwin announced. There was not a cloud in the sky.

They noticed the lightning about an hour after dark. It flashed white in the west, making visible the tremendous line of black-blue thunderheads approaching the camp. There was now an entire crew of cookers that would stay the night with the hog. The world's problems could get solved in one night of hog cooking.

"The fire right?"

"We might add a few more coals to last out the storm."

"Don't add too much. Wayne and Edwin will skin our hides if we burn the porker."

The pre-storm wind came quickly, shooting small sparks from the coal shovel across the grass as Don added heat to the fire. The thunder rolled across the sky.

"Somebody stoke up the coal barrel."

Fifteen minutes later, the rain came in driving sheets. Lightning struck once in the woods to the west, and the power went out in a third of Dickson County. The camp was black. No security lights on the perimeter road. No lights in the main dining hall where a mean game of Rook was in progress. No cabin lights. Blackness. Rain. Lightning. Thunder. Wind.

The majority gathered in the dining hall, leaving a few stranded in their cabins. It was as if the family had been thrown back in time to the days of Greenbriar Wilson when Middle Tennessee was totally black at night, every night. Huddling in small groups on the porch and in the hall, they watched the storm. The rain fell off the roof in wide rivers, and the hot summer air became oddly cold. G.W. was perhaps the proudest of his family that night as they calmly pondered the storm, a family not at odds with the land, but a part of it, not afraid, but respectful, not complaining, but accepting. He felt an arm around his waist.

"Hey, son. You all right?"

"Yes, ma'am." He took her hand.

"Some storm, huh?"

"It's a fine one, Momma. I've always loved them."

"I know. Sometimes they scare me, though."

The rain splashed on the ground at the edge of the porch, creating a fine mist that the lightning would catch, illuminating it in mid air.

"I miss him a lot, Momma. You'd think after five years . . . there were things I never said."

She squeezed his hand and lay her head on his shoulder.

"He knew. I know he felt the same."

Three hours later the sky was clear. The stars shown brightly as the hog cookers were gathered at the maple tree. Most everybody else had retired to the darkness of the cabins. With flashlights and candles, they had hardly been inconvenienced by the power failure. The maple tree crew talked until daylight, eating a separate cooking of ribs while working the main course with just the right amount of heat and family sauce. Their laughter could have been heard by any cabin that had non-sleeping occupants; however, the post storm cool-ness made for spectacular sleeping, so no one was bothered. The cooks cussed and discussed the clear cutting of hardwoods for pine production. Deer management and wild turkey restoration were also addressed. Water quality and politics were mixed with coon dogs and setters, the price of cattle and Ford trucks. They told stories of big fish and hard-to-kill turkeys. They talked of honorable men and scoun-drels, strong women and home-made fried pies. They covered good rifles and old shotguns, trajectories and unexplored land.

At first light, Aunt Mary and Uncle Charles began breakfast in the hall. Wayne promised to watch the hog, if it wasn't already burned up, while the all night crew got some shut-eye. The last whip-poor-will was muted by sunlight as G.W. found his cabin. He crawled in the sleeping bag beside his wife and cuddled closely. The last thing he remembered was the warmth being next to her.

He awoke before noon in a sweat. The summer heat penetrated the cabin, and the sleeping bag was still zipped. The cicadas were sounding in the trees outside the window. Throwing back the cov-ers, he listened, and could hear the children on the lake. The fishing tournament for the kids must be in full swing, he reckoned. He was glad that Trae and David were in charge. The Texans were by far the best diplomats in the family, able to smooth out rule infractions with smiles and laughter. When it came to fishing, these kids were highly competitive.

"Hey, Dad. You gonna sleep all day?" Kary, his oldest daughter, entered the cabin. "Look what I got."

She sat cross-legged in the floor with him. A small snake crawled through her fingers, exploring her hands.

"Isn't he pretty?" she said.

"Red-belly. Where'd you find him?"

"Under some leaves by the cabin."

He rolled over, resting his head on his hand.

"I keep thinking you're going to outgrow catching things. You're almost grown up."

"You started it," she smiled.

"Where's your good-lookin' Momma?"

"Down at the lake. She said to tell you to come down and sit with her. She misses you."

"You be sure and release that snake."

Kary slipped her hand in the sleeping bag and laughed, "How 'bout here?"

"Won't bother me," he smiled. "Wouldn't do much to help your Momma's heart, though."

There were kids spread out for two hundred yards on either side of the swimming dock. Worm boxes and cricket containers dotted the bank, as well as tangled lines, floats, and frustrated parents. Each time a fish was caught, a roar erupted proclaiming it. All fish were measured and weighed.

G.W. saw them from the hill, his wife and sister. They sat with their backs to him, facing the lake. Kristen and Keli sat on the ground facing their mothers. It was a four-way conversation between the girls. Quickly, Keli stood up and moon-walked across the grass. They all laughed. It was amazing to him how strong his bond had become toward his sister. Of all the women he had ever known, heard of, or read about, had he the omnipotent powers to choose fate, she would still be his sister.

He studied the scene below him and reviewed the next few days. They would eat barbecue today until they were sick of it. Tonight they would gather under the cooking tree; hopefully David brought his guitar from Liberty, Texas. Tomorrow the horseshoe, softball, tennis, volleyball, and golf competition would be completed, and the evening would end with the family auction where old family heirlooms would go for high dollars, all donated to next year's reunion.

He would reflect during the family picture taking on who was not present this year. There would be gaps in his heart where they used to be. He also studied their faces, some wrinkled and worn, others fresh and untired. Most, though, were strong despite the hardship lines, and their eyes were clear, looking straight forward. It was a family grown from the land, good Tennessee ground, and their roots went deep, holding tight in the wind.

The last morning, G.W. made his way toward the dining hall, crossing two hundred yards of open field. He crossed small tire tracks in the grass, two ribbons of disturbed dew leading off toward the woods. He changed directions and followed them into the woods on the other side. A dirt path held the fresh tracks.

The wheelchair was parked at the ridge top, and Edwin looked off into the hollow. G.W. paused, wondering about interrupting his privacy, but continued anyway. The big man spoke without turning.

"Mornin'."

"Mornin' . . . y'all staying for the church service?"

Edwin turned his chair around. "Yeah. It's important to me."

The cicadas started up again and a blue jay screamed in the hollow. "It's been good, huh?"

"This family leaves good sign, don't you think?" Ed pondered aloud in his deep voice.

"We try hard, I think," G.W. replied. "Are you all right?"

"I tell you, buddy. Nobody ever said that life was gonna be easy. Yeah, I'm all right."

"Let's go get some coffee, what do you say?"

"I say," Ed smiled. "Let's go get some coffee."

They started off across the grass. In the distance they saw Mitzi, Edwin's daughter, walking across the field with her young son, Zephaniah.

Zeph was two years old, walking with quick steps, hand in hand with his mother. He fell and got up laughing. She lifted him into the air, and the two men could hear the child giggling. The boy's laughter grew louder, and as G.W. walked, he realized that little Zeph's happiness was completely drowning out the electric humming of his grandfather's wheelchair.

Fall

The hunter heard the footstep, a single, quick, weighted sound in the leaves. One step is all he heard. One. His eyes moved, nothing more. He waited, eyes strained, fingers on the bowstring. Pulling back just a bit, he tested the bow's strength, feeling its familiar resistance. He waited for the sound of the next step.

He thought it strange how his mind could work while waiting for the second step. He wondered where the sounds of the earlier steps had gone, how an animal could approach and there be one distinct footstep that suddenly crossed the line of his ear's ability to hear.

    The sound came from his left, just over a small ridge. He knew it was a deer. It had not been a quick, scurrying chipmunk sound or the bouncing gait of a gray squirrel. A single hoofed foot had disturbed the leaves, sending a signal of its presence.

    A slight chilled breeze touched his face. He watched the golden, red oak leaves quivering nervously above him. Opening his nostrils, he tried to find any smell of the deer, searching the air for the sweet, musk scent of its hind legs.

    The deer moved, its approaching footsteps signaling a slow walk. The persimmon tree stood twenty yards in front of the hunter, its fermenting fruit laying abundantly around the trunk, sending its own attraction downwind. He moved his head slightly as the footsteps grew louder, trying to detect movement between the trees.

    The doe moved deliberately toward the persimmon tree. The hunter's first sight of it was her head, low to the ground, emerging from behind a red oak. She stopped, head down, frozen in his vision. Staring, he felt his heartbeat quicken, hoping she would continue into the opening. A blue-jay called behind the deer, its irritating scream echoing in the hollow. She moved again, for the first time allowing the hunter to see the source of the footstep's sounds. Step, crunch. Step, crunch. Step, crunch.

The early morning light bathed the deer as she moved through a sunlighted hole in the forest canopy. He pondered her sleek beauty, noticing the muscles in her shoulder as she walked. The deer stopped, smelled the ground, and found her first orange-red persimmon. Lifting her head, she chewed and quickly looked back over her left shoulder.

While the animal's head was turned away, he raised the bow, came to full draw, and released. It was one fluid motion, no different than the deer's. The arrow flight was a slicing streak in the sun's light. He watched the animal turn in a brown blur, and run, tail down, off the ridge, out of his view. He listened to her footsteps, now fast and loud, an unconcerned placement of hooves, breaking sticks and limbs in their escape. Standing motionless, each sound the deer made had a special meaning to the hunter. Those brief clues lasted only a second, maybe two. They gave him a direction and a reading of the wound, a primeval connection with his prey.

The deer fell in the hollow. Lowering his bow at the sound, the woodsman recognized the death crash of body against leaves. It was the sign he had awaited, the moment he prayed for. Were they with him, that single sound would bring smiles to his children and a shriek of joy from his wife. It made good his hours spent working the bow and straightening the arrow shafts. It accented his careful craftsmanship of hunting points. It meant that for this brief time, he had been blessed with goodness.

He moved his legs for the first time since before daylight, breaking the silence with his steps. Stopping at the persimmon tree, he studied the ground where the deer had eaten. Hoof marks showed where the deer had turned. Fresh droppings, slick, black-green pellets, lay under a turned leaf. On the same leaf was one bright red drop of blood. He kneeled and picked up the leaf, balancing the thick fluid in its autumn spoon. Tilting it, the blood rolled off the edge into the palm of his left hand. Bringing his hand to his mouth, he tasted the blood with his tongue before moving off in the direction the deer had run.

After twenty yards, the blood trail became easy to follow. He walked without concern for the noise his feet made in the leaves, a post-hunt luxury. At the bottom of the hollow was a stream, small enough to jump across, but the deer never made the crossing. She lay with her hind quarters in the moving water, her head uphill. The hunter approached the animal from behind, careful not to let his eyes meet hers. Kneeling at her side, he reached across her face, gently shutting her eyelids with his fingers. The arrow had entered just behind the shoulder, the turkey-feathered fletching protruding from the wound. He offered a prayer for the deer's spirit, this hunter alone with the animal he had slain. The prayers were long in accordance with his grandfather's teachings, offering sincerity and thanksgiving.

Removing his footwear, he eased his feet into the cold water, letting the small stream soothe him. He lay on his back, looking up through the colored leaves. There was a feeling in the bottom of his stomach that haunted him. It came every year at this time, when the leaves changed colors and the air lost its stickiness. It was after the whip-poor-wills stopped calling at night and the frogs quit singing. He tried his best to understand the feeling, the desperation and loneliness of it. The haunting was wind borne, he thought, bringing the spirit of winter to his heart. Maybe the pain of winter was the secret to the mystery. The winds of fall were perhaps a foreboding of winter's pain, the hunger, the old people's sickness, the children's tears, his suffering over the welfare of his family, the uncertainty of the season's power. The leaves in the tree above him rattled with a more powerful wind as if confirming his thoughts. He quickly wanted to be home.

The hunter did not cut the deer. They would use all of it. The entire animal was valuable. He lifted the doe across his neck, letting its legs hang down in front of him. Distributing the weight across his shoulders, he started out, climbing the hill to the ridge that led home.

Behind him at the creek where the deer had fallen, lay the broken shaft of his arrow. The flint point he knapped with a polished deer antler lay touching the water, being washed of its red stain.

Four hundred years later, on a ridge in Perry County, Harrison Grant watched the deer. He had heard it cross the stream in the hollow and followed its footsteps up the hill until it became visible feeding on acorns in front of him. He listened for other footsteps behind her, thinking a buck might be in pursuit, but the only sound was a barge on the Tennessee River some three miles to the west. The deer looked away, and the hunter silently stood in his tree-stand. He brought the bow up and came to full draw. The doe fed thirty yards away, the last rays of the day's sun falling softly on her in the clearing.

It was a good shot, the deer well within range and broadside, but he did not take it. Easing the bow to a relaxed position, he sat, watching the animal feed. He had learned to do that, pass shots. He did not remember when, but his hunting had taken a different turn. It was the time in the woods he valued, and if he returned home with meat for his family, that was good too, but not absolutely necessary.

Today, he was contemplating a feeling, the feeling of fall. It had overwhelmed him since he was a child, and he could never really put his finger on it. His earliest memories of the feeling were while walking to school in the first grade. There was an apprehension in the air, an impression of being overpowered by something unknown. At first he thought it was the newness of school, the excitement of a new situation. Later in life, he realized the feeling came every year and that school was just coinciding with timing of the feeling. It had to do with the change from summer to fall, but more than anything, it had to do with fall.

The deer lifted her head, testing the air. The breeze had shifted, swirling his scent in the ridge-hollow thermals. Harrison Grant watched as she tried to figure the smell, raising her nose high, searching for the escaping hint of danger. She tail-wagged and resumed feeding until out of sight down the ridge.

He left the stand early, wanting to use the last of the light to walk home. The air had already chilled. The temperature was supposed to drop into the thirties. He wondered about the winter, whether the cold would cause a drastic increase in his electric bill, but then he would just make sure the woodburning stove stayed fired up. He pondered new tires on the truck and where the money would come from to fix either of his vehicles if they broke down. They had, between them, over two hundred thousand miles. There were braces needed for Shelia, according to the orthodontist. He hoped they had a payment plan. There was never any extra money and with the economy slumping, no hope for a raise. In the winter, there was always Christmas, an added cost.

The hunter came to the creek in the bottom of the hollow. Pushing off with his right foot, he cleared the water and landed safely on the other side. He continued up the hill, leaving behind the tip of an exposed arrowhead in his boot print. He never knew what he left behind and the meaning behind it, for somewhere between the two hunters was lost the secret of fall's power.

She screamed it to them, so that they felt her calling in the bottom of their stomachs. She sent it on the wind and in the silence of her children. She taught the conquering of apprehension through her own colors, the hope seen through dying leaves, the voices in an October breeze, and the history of our own mortality within her womb.

Winter

Sandy stood in the front yard watching the smoke from the chimney swirl downward, briefly fogging her view of the house. The north wind had a hurt to it. It stung her face, forcing her to shut her eyes against its bite. She wondered about smoke that went down, hot air that sank, contradicting the science text in her book satchel. Tears formed in the corners of her eyes as she stared into the wind at the chimney. She could hear the bus turn onto the main highway, grinding gears and heading back toward town, as her mother appeared at the front window and waved. Sandy hated these short days. It was dark when she boarded the bus in the morning and nearly dark when she got home.

She climbed the last porch step when she heard the coyote. Turning, she looked out over the pasture in front of the house. It was dotted with black cows, moving slowly toward the large hay rolls positioned strategically across the pasture. She watched her father's pick-up move slowly across the field toward the barn and wondered whether he could hear the coyote. It called again, a lonely cry that made her flesh crawl. She wondered if the coyote could stare into the north wind without its eyes watering. The door opened behind her.

"Come on in, Sandy. It's cold out there."

"Yes, ma'am."

Her mother held the door open as Sandy entered the warm house. She dropped her books in the corner behind the door and started to shed her coat.

"In your room, young lady, with the books. Your dad will pitch a fit if he sees them there."

Sandy picked up the books without an argument.

"What's it mean when smoke goes down, Mom?" She dropped her coat on a chair in route to her room with the books.

"Hang your coat up. That's not the closet."

Sandy wondered how mothers could see through walls as the voice came from the kitchen out of her line of sight. She looked forward to the future when she could perform motherly miracles on her own children.

"Smoke, mother. How come it can go down?"

Sandy could hear plates being removed from their cabinets and her mom answering loudly so the words would go around walls.

"The wind, honey. The wind can blow it down."

Sandy rounded the corner of the kitchen. She went straight to the silverware drawer and retrieved enough for the supper table.

"It's more than the wind, Mom. It's something else. I thought hot air rised up."

"Rose. You thought hot air rose."

"Mom. Listen to what I say instead of how I say it. I'm wondering about something here."

"So am I. Whether you're going to grow up with the ability to speak correctly. Just because you live in the country doesn't mean you're stupid. Rised up sounds like you're uneducated."

Sandy stopped setting the table and looked at her mom. She then looked outside at the rolls of hay in the pasture, remembering when she was younger how they reminded her of elephants. She would make believe she lived in Africa.

"I must be uneducated, Mom. I don't even know why smoke goes down."

The back door opened and then shut quickly. Sandy could feel the presence of her father down the hall, and as she placed the last fork, she realized her ability to see through walls was maturing. She knew he was hanging his coat on the rack. She heard the chair scoot across the floor as he sat to remove his boots.

"Daddy! What are you doing right now!"

"Just a second, I'm taking my boots off," came the deep voice down the hall. "I'll be right there."

Sandy smiled.

The male coyote sat at the entrance to his temporary den in the bulldozer pile. He had used it many times before when in the area. As he watched the land in front of him, the north wind moved the hair on the back of his neck. Raising his nose and jerking it to the side, he tried to pick up a scent being whisked along with the wind, but it was gone too quickly. The pain in his stomach urged him to hunt.

He moved through the tall grass, loping easily with little effort. He stopped at a farm road, looking in both directions as if watching for traffic. Turning into the wind, he used his nose again, trying to locate a source of food.

The coyote heard a rustle, a movement in the grass, a non-wind sound. He tilted his head quizzically toward the spot three feet to his right. Flaring his nostrils, he lowered his nose to a position directly downwind. Pulling in a lungful of air, the mouse scent teased his brain. The sound moved. He pounced, immediately feeling frantic movement under his right foot. He bit the ground, feeling the small, wriggling body under his lip. He bit again, but it was gone. Searching with his nose, he frantically sniffed out the escaping mouse in the tall grass. The predator licked his upper teeth feeling the gritting earth that had been trapped there in the attack. His stomach cramped and released. Its emptiness caused him to move in search of something else to make the pain go away.

Sandy opened her eyes, watching her father pray. She knew it was wrong, but sometimes it made her feel good to study him as he said the blessing, eyes closed, callused hands upon the table, talking immodestly to an unseen source of strength in his life. She quickly lowered her eyes as he finished.

The food was passed plate to plate. The wind continued, tossing a metal chime outside the window behind her father's head.

"You think it will snow?" she asked.

"I heard sixty per cent chance," reported the mother.

"That's all I need," he sighed while buttering the bread. "We have calves dropping early which is my fault. That crazy bull. And now cold, snowy weather, and a coyote watching from the sidelines."

Sandy chewed, and swallowed quickly. Her eyes widened.

"I heard him! Behind the north pasture! It's lonely sounding, Daddy. Made spiders crawl in my hair."

He smiled. "Well, maybe he'll find enough to eat that isn't ours. Maybe he'll leave us alone."

A blue-eyed Australian Shepherd sneaked to the table and sat at Sandy's knee, looking up. She eased a piece of roast off her plate and nonchalantly fed it to the dog.

"Old Shep could whip that coyote, couldn't you boy?"

Old Shep licked his lips, easing closer, and laid his head in Sandy's lap. Closing his eyes, he sensed her affection. His belly was full. The wind was mysteriously somewhere outside, not touching him, not making him shiver. The last thing on Old Shep's mind was fighting a hungry coyote.

They finished supper, and the girls cleaned the kitchen while the father stoked the stove. He filled the cast iron kettle with water and placed it on the wood burner. Sandy retreated to her room and reviewed her homework assignments. She studied more on the possibility of snow than her school work, however. From under the bed she found her flashlight and took it to her window. She turned it on trying to pierce the windy darkness on the other side of the glass, but had little luck until turning off her overhead light. Sitting at her window in total darkness, she tried again, this time succeeding in casting a white ribbon of light into the blackness.

At first she was not sure, but by staring intently into the path of light she picked up a quick flicker and then another. They were pioneer flakes, the first to release from the safety of the mother cloud, and Sandy smiled to herself holding back her excitement until they began to grow in their intensity. Faster they came, almost horizontal to the ground, traveling uncontrolled by the wind, until her meager light path was filled with a thousand, maybe a million, fat moving snow flakes.

The father had just reclined in his chair. The muscles in his back rested for the first time since daybreak. He was pondering the absolutely wonderful silence of his den. No television. No radio. No talking. There was just the winter outside and this magnificent chair in his warm house. He shut his eyes and could feel the sleep instantly overcome him as if a doctor had injected him with some powerful drug that would steal away his consciousness. From somewhere in his brain, there suddenly came an excited child yelling "SNOW, DADDY, IT'S SNOWING!"

The coyote turned into the wind. The snow flakes caught in his eye lashes causing him to blink as he stared into the darkness. He knew instinctively that the hunting would be difficult. Few animals stirred during a snow storm, preferring the shelter of wind-blocking thickets and den holes. He could feel the wet coldness of the snow under his feet, seeping between the earth-hardened pads and clumping into small ice balls as he walked.

The ground had frozen before the first flakes had fallen, and the storm's snow accumulated quickly. It was a wet snow that clung to the tall grass and was transferred to him as he passed. By the time he reached the main highway, the hair on his back had turned white covering the brown-black coloration of his pelt.

The coyote stepped into the road. He liked the hard surface where normally he could detect heat from the day's sun, but he felt no warmth now. The ice balls were forced upward into their crevices causing some discomfort in his feet, but he put the minor pain from his thoughts. The cramping in his belly overpowered it. The flat, white road surface extended into the darkness in both directions, and in the distance was one pair of amber, yellow eyes glaring toward him, growing in size and whiteness. He stared at the approaching eyes with no concern for his safety. He checked the side of the road, his escape route, and then returned to the stare as the first sound touched his ears. There was something mysteriously attractive about watching the lights as the sound grew louder, like teasing a rabbit before eating it. He waited until the lights from the eyes fell upon him, before diving off the road into the high grass on the other side. In the second leap, his body fell through where the ground should have been. The water from the ditch enveloped him before his feet touched bottom, and in a single bound he cleared the opposite bank finding the security of the high grass again. He stopped and shook, knocking fresh snow from the grass in a swirl around his head. The wet cold hurt him, a throbbing, dull pain that eased somewhat as he moved.

So, he moved, loping across the field toward a tree line along the creek. The snow squeaked under his feet until he slowed to a walk in the trees. The leaves sounded with each step, the snow muffling the crunch. At the water's edge, he turned upstream and followed the creek until finding a large, exposed root system jutting abruptly over the bank. He turned uphill and entered the snowless cavern below the roots, feeling immediate relief from the windy snow. Sniffing in the tree's blackened cave, he sensed no other animal's presence and entered deeper into the refuge. He lay down. He rested. The creek's sounds made him shiver, starting at the shoulder and extending into his neck. Craning his head upward, the howl came slowly at first, a low, guttural, resonating, musical plea, its source deep in the cramping emptiness of his stomach, continuing much longer than his breath allowed until the coyote was only a shell of the howl, a living instrument that created it. He lowered his nose to the hair at his shoulder and exhaled, feeling the warmth from his breath. Shutting his eyes, he wished he could sleep, but his shoulder would not be still.

Sandy slipped the flannel night shirt over her head. She had just retrieved it from the dryer, and it still held the warmth from the machine. She ran down the hall to her room and shut the door. Grabbing the flashlight, she looked outside again. The snow continued. She shined the light to the ground where the accumulation was approaching three inches. Throwing the flashlight on the floor under her bed, she took off again down the hall. Entering the den, she made a quick pass by each parent, offering a hug and kiss before saying goodnight.

"What are you so happy about?" he asked.

"No school! No school!" she laughed and was gone. The parents looked at each other, smiling.

"Do you remember when life was that simple?"

"Yes," Mom replied. "It doesn't really seem that long ago." They heard the door close to their daughter's room at the opposite end of the house.

Sandy dove into the bed that Mom had already turned back. Her toes were cold in the sheets at the bottom of the bed, and she pulled her knees under her chin. She cuddled deeper into the pillow and pulled the blanket tight around her neck with visions of sunlight on tomorrow's new snow.

Just before sunrise the coyote emerged from under the roots. The storm had passed and the world had become very still. With the wind gone, he felt warmer, but the snow was much deeper. The moon shined on the white ground and his vision was good. He crossed the open field, heading south toward the cow field. Never before had he failed to catch something under the hay where the big animals stayed.

From the top of the ridge he looked down on the field. He could see the big animals gathered around the barn and a few eating at the rolled hay. They stood out against the snow, their dark bodies contrasting sharply with the moonlighted whiteness. Keeping close to the tree line, he skirted the field narrowing the distance to the hay.

He came upon the cow by accident. She had used the cedar tree as a wind break during the storm when her birthing began. It was a difficult birth, her first, and her instincts were confusing to her. She had done motherly things for the very first time, and yet they came naturally, a process of timeless mystery. The sudden presence of the predator so close to her calf terrified her. She snorted and made a false charge at the dog-like animal, leaving her wobbly-legged progeny alone at the cedar. The calf tried to follow her, but fell.

The coyote retreated five steps and began to circle, keeping his eyes on the calf. The cow returned to her calf and began to bellow, immediately prompting the cows in the distance to return her call. He darted in, bringing another charge, but this time he tested her, holding his ground, lips snarled and growling. The Angus stopped short of the coyote, and then moved into the field hoping the calf would follow. Her safety was at the barn. The calf must follow her to the others at the barn. The calf, however, was having trouble standing, its legs shaking from the cold and the fear, and the newness of life.

The coyote saw its opening and attacked, seizing the young calf at the neck. He bit hard and twisted his head instinctively, throwing the calf to the ground. It tried to bawl, but had no air. The cow charged again; the predator refused to move, except to drag the calf backwards toward the fence. The cow, in her fury, trampled them, her right front hoof knocking the coyote sideways and breaking the calf's back.

They stood there, staring at each other. The calf was without movement. She nudged the body, trying to make it stand. Nothing. She nuzzled once more and moved off ten steps, again hoping the calf would follow. The coyote moved again and with a great show of strength, lifted the front half of the calf, dragging it quickly under the fence and into a draw on the other side. Once alone, he fed, filling his aching stomach with newborn calf. He forgot the cold, the storm, the miserable night before. The soothing of hunger pains was his only emotion.

Sandy and her father entered the field as the sun rose slightly above the horizon. The old truck was missing a bit, complaining in its own way about the cold. The snow squeaked under the tires as it rolled along, and Sandy wondered where the sound came from. She smiled to herself, happy to be in the truck with her father, happy with the new snow, happy with the farm and the cows. They stopped at the barn immediately hearing the bawling cow in the fence row. The farmer knew and pulled a Winchester rifle from behind the seat.

"C'mon, Sandy," he said seriously. "We've got a problem."

She had to struggle to keep up with his long steps in the snow. She knew better than to ask questions. There was a tone in his voice she had learned long ago to listen to, without talk.

The cow stood with her tail to them, her head across the fence. Afterbirth hung between her legs and quivered each time she bawled. They saw blood on the snow at her feet.

The coyote had heard the truck enter the field. Leaving the carcass, he walked up the tree line two hundred yards and looked back, his stomach heavy after the feeding. Wanting to cross the field, he studied them approaching the cow. Like his duel with the car lights, he felt safe with the distance and stepped boldly into the field, beginning a gentle lope across the open ground.

The farmer spied him quickly and fell prone in the snow. Sandy stood still and watched. She had seen him shoot often and figured the coyote would die, even at that distance.

The .270 reported and Sandy heard the bullet say "whup" a half-second later. The coyote rolled, was up again, and ran straight out for five steps before dying in mid-stride. He became a distance speck in the snow that did not move. Her father stood without speaking, brushed the snow from his clothes, and moved toward the cow. Sandy followed.

The half-calf lay in the draw across the fence. Snow was red in a five foot circle around it. Sandy stared bravely at the devoured animal, feeling tremendous pity for its short life.

"It's not fair, Daddy," she whispered.

He rested his big hand on her shoulder and squeezed before running off across the field. She turned too, looking twice across her shoulder at the calf in the draw.

They approached the coyote side by side. It lay outstretched like a dog asleep in front of the fireplace. It looked peaceful, she thought, with no pain. The farmer knelt in the snow at its feet. She stood behind her father, placing her hands on his shoulders. He ran his hand across the coyote's side, feeling the long hair in its pelt. A crow called in the distance and another answered. She felt the tears swelling in her eyes, and this time there was no north wind to cause her crying.

"Do you just hate him, Daddy?"

"No," he said flatly. "Not at all."

"But he ate our calf."

"So he did, Missy. He ate the calf."

"It's not fair that stuff like this has to happen."

The crows continued in the distance as the farmer stood. Suddenly, Sandy was uncomfortable with the moment. She needed to say something, but nothing seemed right.

"Daddy, why does smoke go down?" she blurted.

He put his arm around her as they started back toward the barn. "Sometimes," he said, "storms just come."

Sandy thought about that, studying her house on the hill in the distance. It was a great house to live in, she reckoned. She had plenty of food, a lovable dog, a warm bed on cold nights, and the smoke from her chimney was rising straight up into a blue sky.

Spring

Mr. Wayne Richardson awoke exactly one minute be fore the alarm was to sound off. Staring at the digital numbers on the bedside table clock, he wondered how it was possible for the sleeping mind to accurately predict the time. The phenomenon occurred often, to the extent that he placed it outside the realm of random coincidence. He laid his hand on the "alarm off" button, watching the seconds tick down until the sleep-killing bullet would discharge, and with only one second to spare, he gently pressed, watching the seconds proceed with no concern for the disgusting aggravation he had prevented. Time was like that, he sleepily pondered, a heartless parent providing the essence of opportunity with absolutely no emotion.

He turned his head, studying his wife of fifty years, lying comfortably beside him. Her breathing was unlabored and gentle. He wished that once, just once, she would snore, so that he could grab the cassette recorder from under the bed and preserve the occurrence for all future complaints against him. Such a recording would serve to end thirty years of playful, nighttime bantering, and give him the final laugh.

Mary Richardson opened her eyes, meeting his, as if she could feel his thoughts in her sleep.

"You were snoring," he lied.

"I don't snore," she whispered sleepily.

"Were too," he continued. "A big, loud, nasal snore with a couple of quick coughs. I thought you were dying. I don't know how you expect me to get any proper sleep with all that carrying on. You ought to go see a doctor. If you really loved me, you would."

She closed her eyes, cuddling deeper into her pillow.

"Either get up and go hunting or shut up and go to sleep. I'm sleeping, old man, and in no mood to carry on a conversation."

He propped his head on his hand. "Well, it's the only time you don't want to talk, and the only time I can get a word in edge-wise, so come on, old woman . . . talk to me." He reached across the darkness, opening her closed eye with his index finger.

"Would you leave me alone!" she said.

"I remember a time when you were happy to wake up early, when the kids were here and it was the only time we had privacy."

She opened the same eye by herself this time.

"That's when I was young and beautiful. Now I'm old and sleepy."

He closed the distance between them and kissed her on the eye.

"You're still beautiful, old woman, but definitely ornery at four in the morning."

She smiled as he swung his legs off the bed and walked stoop-backed toward the bathroom. Sometime between washing his face and buttoning his shirt, his back straightened to normal and the pain subsided. He finally found the big cotton socks in the drawer and made his way toward the bed, where he sat lightly, not wanting to wake her. The right foot was socked with no trouble, but just after clearing the toes on his left foot, a shearing electric pain sledge-hammered his lower back. It took his breath, only allowing a portion of his lung's air to be used in the exclamation.

"Ahhhhhhh!"

Mary Richardson sat straight up in bed, both eyes open to their widest diameter.

"Wayne! What's wrong!"

Wayne couldn't move, stuck in the ridiculous position of being half-socked.

"Back . . . ," he tried. "Can't move. . . ."

The old woman knee-walked across the bed to her husband, shaking him with each step, causing corresponding groans of pain.

"Will you be still! You're killing me," he puffed with no air.

She climbed off the bed and faced him, her face drawn with worry.

"What can I do, honey?"

"Go in the den and get my shotgun," he whispered.

"What?" she asked.

"Are you deaf? Go get my gun, bring it in here and shoot me."

"What!" she cried.

"You are deaf." He rolled his eyes, but that even hurt and he yelled out again. "You ever heard of putting an animal out of misery? Well, I'm an animal in misery. I've loved you immensely. It's been wonderful, but I'm stuck in a terrible position with no sign of recovery. Shoot me, Tinsey, and make sure of your shot."

Tinsey covered her mouth as she began to laugh.

"Don't you start," Wayne smiled, gasping with pain each time he moved, and she was on the floor laughing. Wayne Richardson was mad and laughing at the same time, unable to perform either emotion properly. Forcing his hands away from his foot, the pain left him as quickly as it had come. He breathed a full breath, testing, and he moved his shoulders, waiting for the pain to return, but he was free. The malady had flown away like an eagle temporarily grasping a fish and then losing its grip.

He finished dressing, not speaking to Mary, who followed him around the house apologizing for her morbid laughter. He secretly understood her dilemma remembering the times she stumped her toe on the bed post while making the bed. He could not help but laugh as she lay writhing on the floor in pain.

"I'll be back by seven," he offered before exiting the back door.

"You are crazy," she preached. "What if it happens in the woods?"

"I'll get more sympathy from the squirrels than you," he responded with the hint of a smile at the corner of his mouth. The door shut behind him.

On the back porch, the awakening spring morning was alive with sound. It was like exiting a silent cave into a stereophonic studio of bird calls. The eastern horizon was a lighter shade of gray and the cardinals were at full volume. A whippoorwill was vocalizing at a desperate pace in the side yard, and he could hear four others in the darkness behind the house. Barred owls were barking and screaming with their eerie repertoire as he closed the back gate and headed east into the cow pasture. Other species were joining in the morning chorus, defining a thousand separate territories with hundreds of distinguishable songs. His pant legs were wet at the ankles from the clinging dew, and he shifted the weight of the shotgun to his right shoulder, while climbing the grade of the hill to his listening spot, that same section of ground where he had started a hundred previous encounters. It reminded him of when a kid, trying to make safe passage to home base. If he could make it to the listening spot without bumping a bird, it was always the first positive step toward a good morning, the first ritualistic omen of superstitious excitement.

He skirted the edge of the timber, approaching home base with extreme caution, each step placed with quiet deliberation. Leaning against the old oak, he viewed the timber expanse before him, a series of sloping ridges and hollows falling gently in elevation to the east. Taking a deep breath, he rested, allowing his heart rate to decelerate as he listened. Much lighter now, the crescendo of the morning's avian overture brought with it the absolute realization of spring. Crows were calling for the first time to the south, doing mock battle with a screaming barred owl.

The turkey gobbled three hundred yards from Wayne Richardson, off a spur ridge to his right. It was a thunderous, rattling gobble achieving immediate dominance. The forest seemed to momentarily pause in respect for the bird's call for authority. The hunter's heart rate quickened, trying to pinpoint the bird's exact location, and the turkey obliged again with a double gobble.

"You shouldn't have done that," Wayne whispered to the bird as he moved quietly from home base toward the bird's roost.

He closed the distance to a hundred yards, taking his time, moving slowly. Figuring the turkey to be roosted on the side ridge, he paused at the juncture, pondering the war plan of calling the turkey back to the main ridge. The bird gobbled three times while Wayne studied the situation, sounding much closer than he had figured. Finding a suitable tree, he opted to set up.

With the slate, the hunter tree-called. The bird gobbled immediately. Wayne shut up and waited, adjusting his position against the tree to achieve the most comfort possible with the gun resting on his knee. Twenty minutes later the bird tore out of the tree with two quick wing beats and a leafy thump. Wayne waited some more, knowing the gobbler had heard his hen yelps. Also, Wayne hated to play the part of a pushy, nagging female, which could give the old boy too much confidence, causing him to wait for the girl turkey to come to him. On the other hand, he remembered, there were those gobblers who really loved aggressive hens, and pumped with hormones, would come running to such flirtations. The old hunter loved that part of turkey hunting, having to read the personality of the bird, and then return the appropriate female conversation that would turn him on. Today, Wayne Richardson chose to play hard to get.

Fifteen minutes later his back had begun to strain from the unmoving position he had maintained. His right leg was asleep from the knee to his toes, and the decision to move for some muscular relief came at exactly the same time he saw the turkey. The top of the gobbler's fan was visible at sixty yards, moving slowly toward the hunter in small, quivering circles. At fifty yards, the bird emerged from behind a blowdown, and Wayne saw the white skullcap. He flicked the safety off and waited for the bird to cover ten more yards, but his right leg was quivering, making it difficult to hold the bead on the base of the turkey's neck.

He scooted his right leg one inch sideways to re-stabilize his position when the back attack came suddenly from behind him, like a great steel claw had emerged from the tree and skewered him to it. He could not prevent the breathtaking exclamation of pain.

"Ohhhhhhh. . . ."

The turkey fell from his strut and quickly transformed from a quivering puff-ball of patriotic colors to a sleek, black running machine.

"PPPERTTT . . . PPPERTTT . . . PPPERTTT," was all Wayne heard before the tremendous bird took three quick steps and disappeared from planet Earth altogether. The hunter managed to put the safety on, but any other movement hurt too badly, so he waited again, frozen in a microposition of painlessness for the attack to subside.

Mary Richardson looked at the clock over the refrigerator. He was never thirty minutes late, and it irritated-worried her. After all, she had just spent the better part of an hour preparing a special breakfast for his return, a peace offering of sorts, for her terrible laughter fit. On the other hand, what if it happens again, her husband frozen in movement like an aging, farmer statue positioned ironically in a lost hollow where no one could ever view him. The mind picture overwhelmed her.

She quickly checked the stove and proclaimed to the house, "Everything is off!" It was a trick she began after turning forty to remind her that she had double checked. Grabbing a light jacket and her walking stick, she ventured outside expecting to see him coming off the hill. Nothing. She yelled his name to the farm. Nothing. And she started in the direction that he always went, having watched his escape route many times before. Finding his boot tracks in the damp mud behind the barn, she continued up the hill through the pasture, bad knees and all.

Mary became winded halfway up the hill, and she paused to rest her heart, as well as her knees. She looked at her watch again. Eight o'clock. She screamed his name, a bit more frantic this time, and a crow answered above her, but that was all. She pressed on, climbing toward the crest of the hill, her eyes searching the tree line for any clue of his presence. At the top, she fought a tearful panic. Before her lay nothing but timberlands, and she had no idea where to go from here. The thought of entering the woods confused her, creating a dreamlike panic of falling.

"WAYNE RICHARDSON! YOU OLD GOAT! WHERE ARE YOU!" she yelled to the forest.

"Hhheeyyy . . . ," she heard faintly in front of her. She covered her heart with a trembling hand at the call. His voice shattered the intimidation of the woods, drawing her into them with a mindful purpose. Walking another hundred yards, she called again.

"WAYNE!"

"WHAT! . . . OHHH!"

She took off again at a feeble trot until she could see a human leg protruding from a tree trunk. Slowing her pace, she circled the tree like a watchful gobbler, exposing bits of the picture with each step, until she was standing at his side, looking down.

"What are you doing?" she asked.

He tried to crane his neck upwards to look at her, but the pain took his breath.

"I'm stuck again," he whispered with a slight grin. "Would you mind taking this gun off my knee?"

She grabbed the shotgun.

"Carefully . . . ," he commanded. "Lay it over there, muzzle pointed away from us."

"I know how to handle a shotgun," she argued, laying the gun safely in the leaves. She found a nearby stump and sat, watching him.

"Are you all right?"

"Yeah," he replied calmly. "Just can't move right now, but it'll pass . . . I hope. If not, there are worse places to die. Except for the muscle cramps, it's been a really good experience. I figure sometimes the Good Lord just grabs ahold of you and makes you stop for awhile."

"You have lost your mind. I am married to a crazy man," she said. "Mother always said it was true."

"Ahhh . . . your mother has nothing to do with this. Come here. Sit by me."

"I'm quite comfortable, thank you," she returned.

"I said get your backside over here and sit by me," he ordered.

"Oh yeah . . . what are you gonna do, old man? I've got you right where I've always wanted you. I may lecture you for the better part of the day. Captive audience, I believe they call it."

He looked at her, seriously. "Come here, Mary."

She smiled and moved to his side, sitting in the leaves at the base of the oak. The sun had risen substantially, warming the ground around them. Mary could feel the warmth on her face as she rested her head against the bark.

"It's amazing . . . ," he started, "what spring does to me. I've been sitting here trying to forget the pain, so I shut my eyes. Shut your eyes, Mary."

Mary looked at her husband and carefully placed her right hand on his leg."

"Are you sure you're all right?" she asked.

"Yes, I even think I can move now."

He slowly moved his left hand away from his knee, taking her hand.

"See, all better. Now, close your eyes."

She obliged, for the first time hearing the woods around her. The birds had lost their first light intensity, seeming to have been settled by the warming sun. The warm rays bathed her eyelids as she became more intense in her listening. A woodpecker hammered. A light breeze rustled the leaves above her. A blue jay screamed and a pileated woodpecker returned the scream. She could hear a beetle of some sorts moving leaves at her feet, and she could feel the strength of his hand. She heard his voice.

"It's alive . . . refreshed . . . cured of the winter oldness." And now he whispered.

"And if you try real hard, Mary, with your eyes closed, just listening to the spring . . . we are young again. My back and your knees and all the wrinkles and tiredness . . . it's gone. Just the sounds and the sun and our hands and our thoughts. There is nothing old here, Mary . . . nothing."

She squeezed his hand, but did not speak and did not open her eyes. He rested his head against the tree and squeezed back, closing his eyes.

From two hundred yards away on the crest of the next ridge, the turkey was watching. He studied the two forms at the base of the tree, and for some sixth-sense reason, detected no danger. He suddenly shook like a dog, fluffing his magnificent feathers. Taking two steps, he stopped, raising his head higher to study the forms again. Quickly, he extended his neck and gobbled, hearing the echoing call in the hollow below.

Wayne Richardson felt his heart pump harder with the gobble, but never opened his eyes, and as the bird moved away in hopes of finding that special female of his roosting dreams, the young hunter smiled.

The Fear Taker

The sun crested, flowing over the mountain and spilling into the Musselshell River Valley in central Montana. It warmed the twenty thousand acres of Stillwater Ranch and all those who worked there. The warming sun was always welcomed, even in the brief months of summer.

Lute, Tom Ed and young Pix heard the faint calling of Canada Geese in the distance. They sat silently around a small campfire, tasting the hot coffee, smelling the woodsmoke. Lute was the oldest, perhaps sixty, his wrinkled face showing the years of tough Montana winters. He studied the kid, sitting across the fire, and spoke in a slow, deep voice.

"Your eyes will fail you, boy, if you keep up this daybreak reading. It's hard to work cows after you've gone blind."

Pix looked up and smiled. "There ain't a lot of time to read on this job, Lute. You work me till slap dark."

"That's what Mr. Goodnight pays me to do," Lute offered.

Pix thumbed through the tattered paperback book, unaffected by Lute's ribbing. Finding the page, he read slowly with some difficulty.

"Here it is. Listen to this. 'We all strive for safety, prosperity, comfort, long life, and dullness. The deer strives with his supple legs, the cowman with trap and poison, the statesman with pen, the most of us with machines, votes, and dollars. This could be good, but too much safety seems to yield only danger in the long run. Perhaps this is behind Thoreau's dictum: In wildness is the salvation of the world. Perhaps this is the hidden meaning in the howl of the wolf, long known among mountains, but seldom perceived among men.'" Pix looked up from under his hat, checking their response.

"Who wrote that?" Tom Ed asked.

"Leopold. Aldo Leopold. Logan asked me to study it and give him my thoughts. It's his book," Pix said, trying to add credibility to his efforts. The other two ranchhands were staring.

"Well?" Pix persisted.

"I didn't know you could read such big words," Lute smiled. He emptied his cup into the coals, causing a sizzling smoke cloud that lived briefly before disappearing above them.

"C'mon, Lute . . . Tom Ed. What's too much safety mean? I'm needin' your thoughts here," Pix said.

The older hands moved to their horses. Pix followed with the book as they tightened their cinches.

"I'd say Mr. Leopold has done some time on a horse. Thoughts like that usually come from the back of a horse," Lute said.

"What's a dictum?" Tom Ed asked.

"I don't know . . . maybe the way he figured something," Pix tried.

Lute leaned forward in his saddle, combing the horse's mane with his fingers.

"Then here's Lute's dictum. If Logan Stroud handed me a book as tall as this horse and said, 'Lute, I reckon you oughta read this,' why I'd start at the first page and go plum through it. That's how much stock I put in the man's advice. But I'd do it on my time, not Mr. Goodnight's."

"But Lute, you can't read a lick," Pix said looking up.

"That's right. I'd learn. Now, you meet us at the river valley shack in two hours with the gear," Lute ordered. "If you're late, I'll teach you about the danger in thinking you're safe."

The two horsemen laughed, moving off at a slow walk, as the sun became fully visible over the mountain. Young Pix stood watching, perplexed over the idea of too much safety.

Karen Collins took her eyes from the road and briefly watched her son sleep. His hairless head bounced on the pillow with the corresponding bumps in the dirt road. He was small for his ten years of age, and even in his sleep, she could detect his worry, a small wrinkle between the brows, a visible air of concern behind his closed eyes. The tears came suddenly. She was used to it. When she was alone or he was asleep, she would allow them to flow freely, but never in his awakened presence. She must be brave. She must always be positive, the doctors had lectured. She held his hopes for a future like a wilting flower in her hand, and she could not nurture it to strength. And so she cried, driving on a dirt road in Montana, a long way from Nebraska, because there was simply nothing else to do. She had even stopped praying.

Karen had heard about Logan Stroud from a friend of a friend of a friend their last day at the children's hospital. A Tennessean, the man had said, who worked on a cattle ranch in Montana, who had a special gift with terminally ill children. He did not cure them. He made no claims as a healer. This man, this Tennessean in the Rockies of Montana, simply took their fear away. The story was that he had total success. No child had ever left him with a fear of dying, but on the other hand, no child could explain it either. So, in a last desperate attempt to soothe her son's heart, she begged days off from her boss, withdrew the last bit of savings from the bank, and headed northwest. She wiped her eyes with a Kleenex.

"I must be crazy," she whispered to herself.

"What?" Zach said half-asleep, rubbing his eyes.

"Good morning," Karen said cheerfully. "Boy, are you a sleepyhead."

"Are we there yet, Mom?"

"That nice policeman said it was on this road," she replied.

"Did you see how he smiled at me, Mom? When we asked how to get to Stillwater Ranch, this big smile came over his face. Are all people out here that nice? Wow! Look, Mom. The mountains!"

Topping a hill, the valley lay below them, butted against the base of the mountains. The entrance sign to Stillwater Ranch rose high above the road suspended between two massive tree trunks. An old log house looked over the pasture in the distance. Cattle dotted the fields around the house.

"Wow is right," Karen said, stopping the car so they could take in the scene.

"Do you think your friend is here?" Zach asked, sitting up straight in the seat, leaning against the dash.

"I sure hope so," she answered, letting the car roll forward.

In the house, Mrs. Goodnight wiped her hands on her apron, as she looked out the kitchen window at her husband in the yard. He rubbed his bald head as he talked, as if searching for hair that had long since departed. Mr. Goodnight was getting fat, she thought, and that was good. They had grown old and fat together. She barely heard the knock at the front door.

Opening the front door, her eyes were immediately drawn to the child, white and frail, standing at the tree in the front yard, wearing a baseball cap that was way too big.

"Hello, Mrs. Goodnight?" Karen hoped.

Mrs. Goodnight's eyes moved to the source of the sound directly in front of her.

"Yes."

"My name is Karen Collins. I'm looking for Logan Stroud. I was told he worked here."

"Come in, child. You want a cup of coffee? Tell the boy to come in too."

Karen smiled and lowered her voice. "Could we talk first, in private?"

"Sure." Mrs. Goodnight put her hand on the young mother's shoulder and guided her into the room. They continued into the kitchen. The room was huge. Large cooking utensils hung from a rack over an island stovetop and table. Karen watched as the woman poured the coffee.

"I told Zach that Mr. Stroud was an old friend. I lied. I . . . uh . . . feel really stupid, Mrs. Goodnight."

"Why's that, honey?"

"I don't even know if he's real. I just drove away with no plans. I didn't check on anything. . . ."

And Karen Collins was crying again. She tried to hold it back, but her throat wouldn't let her. Mrs. Goodnight sat in a chair across the table. She smiled, while pouring her own cup.

"Isn't it strange," she whispered. "I don't think you're stupid at all. The thought never entered my mind. What I was thinking was that it must take tremendous strength to do what you have done."

"Desperation," Karen laughed between sniffs. "Pure desperation. I want you to know that I have a good job. People who know me say I'm level headed. *I don't do things like this.*"

Mrs. Goodnight quickly rose from the table and returned from the counter with sugar. "Look at my manners," she said. "You want some milk, honey? Living around here with nothing but cowhands, I forget about anything but black coffee." Karen added the sugar and stirred. The only sound in the room was her spoon against the sides of the cup.

"He's so afraid." She teared again, placing the spoon on a napkin. "I'm sorry. I can't quit crying," she said madly. "He knows. He knows he's dying."

Mrs. Goodnight wiped her eyes with her napkin and smiled. "We cry a lot around here since Logan came. That was seven years ago, you know. He came rollin' in here in a broken down Ford truck with a saddle and a smile. Hailed from some place called Primm Springs, Tennessee, and honey, he had the accent to go with it. Said he always wanted to work in the mountains. Said he didn't know much about cows, but was good with a horse. Mr. Goodnight hired him right off."

"Then he does exist," Karen smiled.

The backdoor opened quickly, and Karen jumped from the sudden interruption. Mr. Goodnight barged into the room as if in the middle of a past conversation.

"Mrs. Goodnight, I found a new bronc buster . . . Howdy, Ma'am . . . yessir, he's just what I was looking for. Big ornery feller and tougher'n boot leather. C'mon in and meet the wife!" he yelled out the back door.

Zach Collins walked into the room wearing a cowboy hat that covered the entire top of his head and eyes. He bounced off a wall and fell. Quickly getting up, he tilted his hat back, walked over to Mrs. Goodnight, and tipped the hat brim.

"Howdy, Ma'am, it's a real pleasure to meet you. Word on the range is that you make a good biscuit." He looked back at the big rancher. "Did I do that right?" he asked.

Mr. Goodnight horselaughed. Mrs. Goodnight covered her mouth as she giggled, and Karen Collins watched in amazement, trying to figure how in such a short time they could feel this comfortable in a strange place so far from home.

Mrs. Goodnight led them upstairs to the guest bedroom. She showed them the bathroom and where the towels were kept.

"We didn't expect this, Mrs. Goodnight. I really don't know what to say."

Zach climbed on the big bed and fluffed a pillow, as Mrs. Goodnight opened a small door leading onto a second story balcony. Karen followed, suddenly overcome with the view from the room. There was a cool breeze coming off the mountains, cleaning the air in the house.

"Mr. Goodnight and I never had children, you see. I prayed and prayed, but it just never happened. And now, in my old age, I'm blessed with children every now and again. They come from all over, and I'm proud of all of them, like they were really my own."

"And they are all sick," Karen whispered.

"No. Some of my children have been sick," the old woman said. "Others have suffered a great pain, but aren't sick." They looked back into the room at Zach, who had already fallen asleep on the bed.

"But I thought. . . ."

"You are my child, too," Mrs. Goodnight said. "God bless you, Karen, for all you've been through, and all your tears, and for coming all the way up here to help this child."

She held the young mother of Zachary Collins, who hugged the old woman back, and they stood on the balcony crying. And it was all right to cry because the sick child was sleeping.

"I don't understand any of this," Karen finally whispered.

"This place is nothing more than it seems," Mrs. Goodnight said. "My husband's great-grandfather started this ranch. We are ranchers. These men here work like most people will never know. We are very simple people. We work hard, and we laugh when we can. We are happy to work, struggle, work some more, and laugh now and then. In the last few years, we have been blessed with a goodness, and that goodness has brought us people like you. When you come, we shift priorities. It becomes much more than a ranch."

"Where is Mr. Stroud?"

"He's been out for three days. He'll be back this afternoon. Don't hurry. Don't worry. Just rest and make yourself at home.

Logan Stroud was dusty, hot and sweaty. He studied on why a horse never smells any worse the dirtier he gets, but a man gets riper the

THE FEAR TAKER • 123

longer he stays away from water. Go figure, he thought. The horse feet made solid swish-clumps through the mountain valley grass as they continued toward home. It was peculiar how three men could ride for ten miles without so much as a decent paragraph spoken between them. Three men. Three horses. And the swish, clump, swish, clump of the animals' feet under them. Three separate man thoughts, three separate horse thoughts, traveling together in complete harmony, like a silent, melodious chord that played unheard between them.

He often thought about Tennessee, so far away from here. It bothered him at first, not being able to get back quickly if needed. Then one day the reality of Tennessee just slipped away, becoming a favorite memory, lost somewhere between the present and a dream of the old homeplace. He remembered the fall mostly, the color of hardwoods in October, the smoke of dark-fired tobacco laying like a fog in the hollows, the call of the barred owls, the smell of hickory burning in a campfire, and the fluttering explosion of a Tennessee covey under his feet. He missed his mother's homemade fried pies, the music of hounds running at night, banjos and flat top guitars.

He wished he could know the thoughts of these men he rode with, if his thoughts were somehow kin to theirs. They were hard men to get close to, especially old Lute, and it had been several years before he understood their soft spoken silence. They just didn't talk a lot, which made you listen when they did. If there were a more fair, hardworking, more principled group of people on earth, Logan Stroud figured it would take a spell to find them.

They all saw Mr. Goodnight at the same time, sitting on his horse at the far end of the valley. Sometimes the old man would do that when they had been out for several days. Riding a mile or so in their direction, he would wait and then they would all ride in together. There would usually be more talk in the last mile than in the three days previous. Usually.

"Mr. Goodnight," Lute smiled.

"Lute. Tom Ed. Logan. Any problems?"

"Nosir. We repaired the well at Butte Creek and rode the fence to Skullbone. If the kid makes it back without wrecking the truck or blowing an engine, we'll be OK," Lute reported.

"We miss anything exciting?" Tom Ed asked.

"Castleman came and picked up his load, and the tractor was delivered this morning. Odds and ends. Logan, you have an old friend from Nebraska here to visit."

Logan smiled. "Sir, I've never said the word Nebraska, much less have any friends from there."

They all laughed. "Well, that's what the mother told her son. She didn't know how to play it. He's about ten, I'd guess. A sick little puppy."

"I see," Logan said. "Have they waited long?"

"No. This morning. Mrs. Goodnight has been taking real good care of them. You know how she is . . . you'd of been proud," Mr. Goodnight said.

"What's my friend's name?"

"Karen Collins," the rancher said. Swish, clump. Swish, clump.

"I'm always proud of Mrs. Goodnight, sir. I'm proud of this whole outfit." And Logan Stroud nudged his horse, galloping away from the others, heading home. The others watched him leave. Three men. Separate wandering thoughts.

"We have a tough day tomorrow," Mr. Goodnight stated. "Do I need to pull somebody over to take his place?"

"Nosir. Tom Ed and I will take up the slack. Logan'll catch up," Lute said.

"That's a fact," Tom Ed added.

"Guaranteed," Mr. Goodnight nodded.

Two hours before sunset, Karen and Mrs. Goodnight drank lemonade in the back yard. Zach was asleep again, tiring quickly after only short excursions with Mr. Goodnight on the ranch.

Karen saw him standing fifty yards away, looking toward the house.

He held the reins in one hand, the buckskin horse standing patiently behind him. He wore a white, long sleeve shirt and was deeply tanned. He stood tall and slender.

"Why don't you go talk to him?" Mrs. Goodnight urged.

"Is that him?"

"I'll go check on young Zachary. Maybe wake him up . . . get him ready," the old woman said.

"Ready for what?" Karen asked.

"They'll be leaving shortly." Mrs. Goodnight rose from her chair and left Karen Collins alone. Standing, Karen noticed her knees trembling a bit. She crossed the yard toward the big tree where the man and his horse were waiting.

Logan Stroud watched her walk. Her arms crossed her chest, like she was chilled. She was slightly out of breath when she reached him, but had climbed no hill. She tried to smile, but failed.

"Hi."

"Ma'am, I'm Logan Stroud."

"Karen . . . Collins," she said. Extending her hand, he took it. She had never touched a hand like his. Hardened with calluses, it was scarred with cuts and scratches.

"My old friend from Nebraska," he smiled.

"Yeah, I guess we ought to get our story straight in case he asks."

"Let's walk. Sometimes it's easier to talk when you walk. Have you ever noticed that?" he said.

"Yes," she breathed easier. "Yes, I have."

They walked slowly, the horse at his right shoulder and the mother from Nebraska at his left. There was no direction, just steps in the mountain pasture.

"I had you pictured differently," she said.

"How's that?"

"I don't know. Just different. You're much more real than I thought."

"Real?" he laughed.

"Yeah, I had visions of this flashy cowboy who performs magic on children. Did you ever see the movie, *The Electric Horseman?* You know with lights and sequins."

"No . . . I don't wear lights. Probably short out real quick," he smiled.

She lowered her hands to her side, walking easier. The horse swatted flies with his tail.

"That's a pretty horse."

"Well, thank you, but he's sort of ugly really. Kinda mule nosed and short legged, but I guess he's the best workin' horse I've ever ridden. A lotta heart."

"My son's got a lot of heart, Mr. Stroud."

"I'm glad of that," he said.

They stopped. He tossed the reins over the horse's head. The animal immediately began pulling grass, feeding along side of them.

"If you don't perform magic, Mr. Stroud, then what is it you will do to help my son."

"I don't do anything, ma'am. I'm just a trail guide for sick kids. You let me have your son 'till daylight tomorrow. He'll come back smiling, and he'll change your life and everybody he touches until he dies. You trust me on this. I won't let you down, ma'am."

She stared at him, searching for an inconsistency, a flaw of insincerity, but it was not there.

"Why won't you tell me exactly what's going to happen? Why's that, Mr. Stroud?"

"Because if I said it, you wouldn't understand it. Your eyes have never seen, or your ears heard, or your heart felt what's ahead."

"And you have?"

"No, ma'am. But I've been there when they have."

They heard the horse approaching and turned to see Mr. Goodnight and Zach. They rode double, with Zach holding the reins in front of the big rancher.

"Logan Stroud, meet Zach Collins," Mr. Goodnight said as the horse stopped. Logan looked at the boy and smiled. He shook hands with Zach.

"How you doin', Zach?"

"OK."

"You reckon he's tough enough to be my partner on this job, Mr. Goodnight?"

"Guaranteed," he replied. "Mrs. Goodnight packed you some grub and blankets." He handed down two cotton sacks. Then he lifted the boy down who quickly went to his mother's side. Logan placed the sacks behind his saddle and turned to the boy.

"Zach, would you mind riding old Buck here?"

"Nosir," he said with big eyes. "By myself?"

"That's right. Kiss your mom. We're wastin' time. We got work to do."

Zach hugged his mom's neck and ran to the horse. Logan lifted him into the saddle and turned back to his boss.

"Take care of my old friend from Nebraska, Mr. Goodnight. I'll take care of Zach."

"Done," Mr. Goodnight smiled.

"Logan," Karen said. He turned to her. "I always did like real better than flashy."

Logan tipped his hat. "We'll see you in the mornin'. Hey, Zach! Can you sing?" He turned the horse, leading it away from the others. Karen heard her son answer, holding tightly to the saddle horn.

"Sure, I can sing."

"Well, good. Ol' Buck likes singin'. It makes him smile. You ever seen a horse smile, Zach?"

"Nossir."

"Well, he's real quick about it. . . ."

They watched them walk away, the bald, whitened sickly boy sitting on a smiling horse and the trail guide who was guiding much more than their direction into the mountains.

"He has good eyes," she said, wiping tears. "Do you believe in angels, Mr. Goodnight?"

Mr. Goodnight smiled. He took a deep breath of mountain air.

"The Bible says that all children have their own angels who visit the Father regularly."

"I asked if you believed in angels."

"Yes, ma'am, I do. I surely do."

Zach and Logan continued into the mountains for an hour. Rising in altitude, they crossed small meadows and fast-flowing streams. They saw mule deer and elk, coyotes and porcupines. Wild flowers were in full bloom, giving a wonderful purple-blue hue to the greenery of the late afternoon.

"Where are we going?" Zach finally asked.

"A bit further. It's a special place that I take special friends. We'll build a fire, cook supper, and after dark, we'll watch for shooting stars."

"I have leukemia," Zach said matter-of-factly. "I'm going to die soon."

"Really?" Logan said without alarm. "I have a real bad ingrown toenail. It hurts me real bad sometimes."

Zach giggled. "That's nothing, Mr. Stroud. A bad toenail isn't bad. It doesn't mean anything, no offense."

"Well, it hurts. That's something, isn't it?"

Zach laughed, leaning forward toward the man walking beside him.

"It won't kill you. Cancer'll kill you. Nobody ever died from a bad toenail, for goodness sake."

Logan stopped the horse and looked back up at the boy. He took his hat off and rubbed his head.

"Now wait just a second, Zach. You mean to tell me that dying is what makes the difference in whether a pain is bad or not?"

"Well, yeah. Everybody knows that."

Logan shook his head. "Not up here, they don't. Cause it ain't true. Shoot, Zach, people and animals have been dying up here for years. Everybody does it. I bet your cancer don't hurt as bad as my big toe."

"You want to bet?" Zach said defensively. "Your toe isn't anything. Look here. I'm bald. Ten years old and I'm balder than Mr. Goodnight."

"So."

"So! You ought to see the way the other kids look at me! That hurts worse than your old toe," he said.

Logan laughed and it echoed off the mountain. He moved to his saddle bag, removed a kit, and lifted Zach from the saddle. They walked twenty yards to the edge of the creek, where he placed Zach on a large rock.

"You sit right there and watch. I don't know where you've been, but you've missed something. Where you been, the moon?"

"No, . . ." Zach laughed.

Logan removed his hat and knelt at the edge of the water. He dipped his head into the cold creek and promptly lathered his head with a bar of soap. He then pulled out a straight razor from his kit and a small mirror.

"Here, hold this," he ordered.

"What are you doing!" Zach yelled.

"Be still! Hold that mirror still, or I might cut my ear off or something."

Logan Stroud shaved his head while Zach laughed. He kept his hair, wiping the blade on his hand. When he finished, he went to the creek and washed the soap out of the harvested hair. Bringing it back to the rock, he showed it to the boy.

"Look here. You say my toe ain't nothing. I say this hair ain't nothing. Look me in the eyes."

They stared each other in the eyes. "In there . . . behind your eyes, that's something. This . . . it don't mean nothing."

He took the hair back to the water and released it. The hair from his head floated downstream and away from them. Rising, he felt the smooth skin on his head.

"The only bad part about it is that my hat probably won't fit right now. Ain't we something, balder than two onions," he smiled.

"I like you," Zach said. "You're OK, Mr. Logan."

"So are you, Zach. You just don't know it yet."

By the time the sun was setting over the mountain, they had built a fire in the back of the meadow. Logan had cooked some bacon for their sandwiches with fresh tomatoes. They finished and smiled at each other, one bald head to another.

"This is fun," Zach said. "But it kind of makes me sad."

"Why's that?"

"Cause when I die, I won't have fun anymore."

"Does it make you sad or afraid?"

Zach grew silent. He started to talk, but stopped. He stared into the fire, and Logan watched as his little head began to shake. His mouth opened and his eyes squenched closed, before the first tears began. His entire body shook.

"I don't want to die. I don't want to. I don't want to," he cried.

Logan Stroud moved to the boy and picked him up. He held him close, feeling his jerky sobs on his shoulder. Holding him tightly, Logan shut his eyes, remembering. He could hold this child, but it was not always so. The memory of it came quickly, like a star shooting across the Montana sky.

The steering wheel was pressed against his chest and he could barely get a breath. The rain come through the broken windshield, chilling his face. His legs were crunched unnaturally underneath him, and the pain in his back seared his brain. He heard her whimpering behind him, quick, breathless sighs of pain. He tried to move, but couldn't. He yelled her name. Nothing. Nothing but quick gasps, and then a faint, "Daddy." He screamed in the darkness, but could only free his right arm. Extending it behind him, he felt for her, finally finding a small hand between the twisted metal. Her fingers tightened around his thumb. He would never in his life forget her fingers wrapped tightly around his thumb.

"Daddy, Daddy, Daddy, Daddy," she whimpered. It was the fear in her cries that he remembered the most. The fear. The horror of her fear overwhelmed him. His helplessness maddened him. Between his sobs, he prayed, loud into the blackened, rainy night, for her fear to be taken away. Please. Please. Take her fear away. And before he passed out, he

thought he heard a voice behind him and the sound of his daughter's laughter.

"Who are they?" Zach whispered in Logan's ear, breaking the memory. The Tennessean paused.

"What do you see?" Logan whispered to the back of his head.

"A man, riding on a red horse. He's standing in the green trees below us. And behind him are red horses, speckled horses, and white horses."

Logan did not turn to see, but lowered Zach to the ground. From behind him he heard a man's voice.

"Zachary, I'll show you."

Zach looked up at Logan. "I want to go," he whispered.

"You're not afraid?"

"No."

He watched as Zach walked away into the dusk toward the evergreens in the bottom. When it was fully dark, he built up the fire. He prepared a comfortable seat using his saddle as a backrest and watched for shooting stars.

The first star shot across the sky like a comet, and before the tail had disappeared from the blackness, he heard their laughter. They were riding horses in the darkness, from one side of the mountain across the sky to the other. Their laughter echoed off the land and flowed downhill toward the ranch house. Between the bursts of laughter were jubilant voices, excited and full of life. Children. Boys' and girls' voices were everywhere in the valley, sometimes in song, silencing the nightbirds and coyotes. Their voices continued long into the night, until Logan Stroud was asleep, his slickened head resting against the cool leather of his saddle.

Karen Collins watched the sun come up over the mountains. She stared in the direction they had departed, from under the tree behind the house. She did not notice at first, but others were gathering at the house. Ranch hands mostly from Stillwater were present, but pickups from other outfits arrived. Mrs. Goodnight had brought a pot of coffee outside, and when Karen looked back at the house, a crowd of people were clumped together in the back yard. From the tree, she wondered about the occasion. Turning back to the mountain, she saw the horse in the distance, walking slowly.

By the time the horse was near, the crowd had joined her on the hill. They all came by, introducing themselves and offering their friendship in subtle ways, a handshake, a hand on her shoulder, a smile. Mrs. Goodnight stood by her, watching.

"What's happening here, Mrs. Goodnight?"

"Become kind of a ritual. We just like to greet them the next morning."

Logan slipped the boy to the ground and let him walk the last thirty yards. Zach ran to his mother amongst the cowboys. She held him close, not knowing what to say.

"Did you have fun?" she asked.

He stood back and looked at her. "It's so simple, Mom. I don't know how we missed it."

"Missed what . . . ?"

"Karen," Logan said.

She looked up to see him standing there, holding his hat in his hand, his bald head shining in the early morning sun.

"Your hair!" she laughed.

"It's gone," he said. "Never used it much anyway. You were right, by the way . . . plenty of heart."

"I know," she said. "I know."

They loaded the car that afternoon. Karen couldn't understand it, but Zach was in a big hurry to get home.

"You don't understand, Mom," he had said. "I've got lots to do."

It was difficult to say goodbye to the Goodnights. They felt the pain, too, in leaving. Logan came down at the last and stood by the car. Zach shook hands with Mr. Goodnight and hugged the old woman's neck. He faced Logan Stroud, looking up into his face.

"C'mon over here," he ordered, taking Logan by the hand and dragging him into the yard. Logan kneeled down so they could be eye to eye.

"What is it, Zach?"

"Well, I didn't know when to tell you, cause I'm gonna cry when I tell you, and I don't want you to think I'm sad."

Logan smiled. "Shoot, cryin' don't mean nothin'. It's not bad. My horse even cries sometime."

"I saw . . . ," and the tears came and his lips trembled. His words quivered through tearful gasps. "I saw Lori and you didn't tell me about her and now I know how much you hurt, and why you do this for kids like me. They're all there, every kid you ever helped. And they all said to tell you they love you and they're all so happy."

Logan Stroud grabbed the boy and held him close as the others watched from the car. He felt Zach's hand reach for his. The boy held the rancher's hand in front of him, studying the cuts and scratches. The tears fell from his cheeks into the Montana grass.

"She said to grab hold of your thumb and squeeze it real tight, and say 'I love you, Daddy.'" And Zach squeezed, looking straight in the eyes of the fear taker.

"No fear," the boy said. "No sickness."

Karen Collins turned onto the dirt road, leaving the Stillwater Ranch in her rear view mirror. She drove a short distance in silence.

"Zach, you have to help me. This has been like a dream. I know you can't talk about it, but what happened up there?"

Zach thought for a second before answering.

"It was night, Mom. I saw a man riding on a red horse, and he stood in the green trees below us. Behind him were red horses and speckled horses and white horses."

"What does that mean?" she asked.

"Stop the car," he said.

Thinking him sick, she quickly pulled to the side. Zach got out and ran around to his mother's side of the car, opening the door.

"Come here," he ordered, grabbing her hand and pulling her

into the road. There was no traffic on the remote Montana road. He took her hand and ran it over his slick head.

"Feel that?" he asked. "It don't mean nothing. I'm sick as a dog, Mom. I don't feel good at all. I'm dying, Mom. And you know what?" He smiled real big. "It's OK. Everything is just the way it's supposed to be. Now you trust me, Mom, cause sometimes a kid knows things that grownups don't."

Zachary Collins died on the twenty-fourth day of November. The funeral was attended by hundreds of kids in the small Nebraska town. They came from all over. None of them cried at the service, because he had grabbed each of them by the hand at one time or another and said, "Come here."

Karen Collins made it fine through the service. He had made her promise to be tough, like Montana ranch hands. She listened intently to the minister, taking great comfort in his words. At the end he had taken a slip of paper from his pocket.

"Zach gave me this paper near the end. It says: 'Please read this for my Mom. She will understand. It will answer the questions she has asked me, that I didn't know how to answer. Zechariah 1, verses 8, 9, and 10.'"

He lay the paper on the pulpit and picked up his Bible. He looked straight at Karen Collins and read.

"I saw by night, and behold a man riding upon a red horse, and he stood among the myrtle trees that were in the bottom, and behind him there were red horses, specked, and white. Then said I, O my Lord, what are these? And the angel that talked to me said unto me, come, I will show thee."

Part II

TOWN CREEK

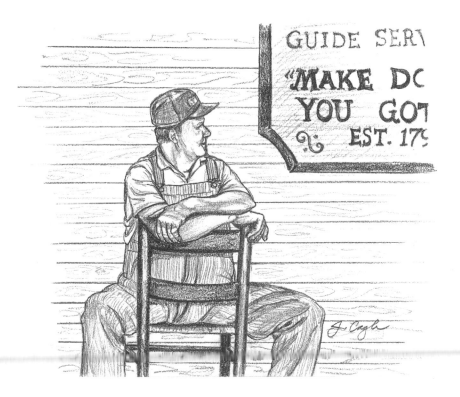

Town Creek
Trading Company

The historical marker on the outskirts of town was the pride of some five hundred inhabitants of Town Creek, Tennessee. It simply stated:

Town Creek, Tennessee, was one of the earliest settlements along the Cumberland River. Founded in 1799, it was the result of river trading and the establishment of the Town Creek Trading Company. Herbert Dawes (1778–1856) was the founder.

Now, to have a historical marker as the only monument to a town as old as Town Creek would bother most folks, but not the Town Creek citizens. They took a certain amount of pride in their obscurity. The fewer people who knew of their town, the less interference they would have in their favorite pastime: living. Outsiders were always a burden to their lifestyles, even kinfolk who came to visit, mainly because of the questions they would ask about the townspeople's priorities, but visitors were handled very tactfully. Questions were ignored as if the person requiring the information were crazy. Persistent questions often led to the interviewer being left alone, talking to the trees. But then the citizens of Town Creek had had fine teachers on life's priorities.

Town Creek was an absolute democracy. All decisions were the results of town meetings and the majority ruled. They had no mayor because they had all agreed that the establishment of political positions would result in professional politicians of which they had no need. They had no sheriff, figuring the citizens could enforce the town rules by themselves, thank you very much. Besides, they had their local wildlife officer to take care of the serious violations in the area. For to the people of Town Creek, serious violations were considered to be those against the land and its wildlife.

Of course, the lack of a sheriff did not indicate a lack of laws in Town Creek. In fact, there were quite a few. For example, drinking was allowed in Town Creek, but drunks were not. If one drank too much and became inebriated, the penalty was silence. Drunks were not allowed to converse with anyone. Punishment for talking while drunk was simple. The drunk was barred from any town function for one month. Herbie McCintosh, to make a point, had not spoken more than a few sentences for the better part of four years. He was, however, allowed to come to all social gatherings.

Herbie had learned to become a quiet drunk. The silence had almost cured him of the bottle until the night he fell in the road and got bitten on the wrist by a copperhead snake, which he said was enough to send him back into the pits of his bottle. Truth was, as most folks knew, Herbie got drunk first and then tried to handle a perfectly defensive copperhead which did bite him, causing him to fall in the road, but the result of the encounter suited everyone better anyway. Herbie was more socially acceptable as a quiet drunk than a sober citizen, and for a good reason. When sober, or at least the last time most folks could remember, Herbie tended to have a one-track mind. He would go on and on about all the reasons his catfish catch was falling off, and since Herbie was a commercial fisherman, a decreased catch lowered his cash flow, which in turn lowered his alcoholic intake. His reasons for decreased catch rates oscillated from sun spots to environmental conditions in the river, which he had read about in a Nashville newspaper. People got real tired of Herbie's theories, and, therefore, appreciated his silence.

The importance of social gatherings in Town Creek cannot be overemphasized. To be banned from social functions was absolutely the worst possible punishment, perhaps due to the closeness of the people or perhaps the uniqueness of their priorities. For example, Suzie Wattly did her senior term paper on the "Entertainment of Folks in Town Creek," which won her a gift certificate at Linda's Seed and Apparel Store. The average citizen of Town Creek watched television an average of two hours a day, according to Suzie's report, and 65 percent of the viewing ended at 7:00 A.M. just after Ralph Emery's morning show. The public simply wished to retain the old ways of entertainment: public interaction. Suppers, horseshoe pitching competitions, softball, shooting matches, porch-swing debates, and church were all important to the citizens of Town Creek. And to think that soap operas and "The Wheel of Fortune" could compete was just downright insulting to their ideas of intelligence.

If social events were the soul of the Town Creek citizenry, then the Town Creek Trading Company was its heart. It was the largest single building in town and the oldest. Since its original construction around 1800, it had burned four times, the last time around 1950, but the Dawes boys always rebuilt it, with additional space for their new enterprises. Presently, it was a two story, wooden building sitting quietly along the bank of Town Creek. It had a large front porch that extended its entire length, with plenty of chairs for its customers.

The sign that hung on the front of the store was artistically painted
and added an antiqueness to its appeal, which fit right in with the
priorities of the town itself. The sign read:

TOWN CREEK TRADING COMPANY
GUN TRADING—WOODROW DAWES
FISH BUYING—STUMPY DAWES
FUR DEALING—BLUE TOOTH BILL
(SEASONAL)
SMALL ENGINE REPAIR—OSCAR DAWES
&
GUIDE SERVICE—TAL DAWES

"MAKE DO WITH WHAT YOU GOT"
EST. 1799

Woodrow Dawes was the unspoken president of the Town Creek
Trading Company and the unspoken father of the town. It was
Woodrow who studied on things deep enough to provide answers
that maintained the integrity of the Town Creek philosophy on living. He was a big man and could back up his decisions with action
when riled, but mostly he shied away from getting riled. He figured
that at fifty years old he should do his best to work things out peace-
ably, if possible. Peaceful solutions, he had found, were harder to
accomplish and therefore more of a challenge to his spirit of sporting
administration.

Andrew Dawes thought about his Uncle Woodrow as he walked
up the steps to the Trading Company. For sure, he'd never known
anyone like his uncle, but what did he know about anything. Andrew
figured that at nineteen, and especially coming from some place called
Town Creek, he was in no position to call himself an authority on
anything. But he did know one thing: he was going to miss the old
man and all the rest of his uncles, too. Andrew just wasn't real sure
about leaving, but he couldn't quite figure out why. He stopped on
the porch and sat in a rocker, waiting before opening up the shop

doors. The rocker moaned as he moved, but he did not notice. Somewhere in the distance he heard a blue jay screaming, but it only touched his consciousness, pestering his thoughts about leaving.

The door opened behind him. Tal Dawes stood in the doorway, occupying most of the doorless space. He held a steaming mug of coffee and looked down at his younger nephew.

"Awful early to be in such deep thought, don't you think?"

"Yessir, Tal," the boy answered. "Sure am glad it's you and not Woodrow here so early. He'd be griping 'cause I was restin' before I ever got started."

"Shoot," Tal groaned. "Any fool can see you're not restin'. Why your head's a spinnin' you're thinking so hard. At least you know what time of day's the best for studying."

Andrew stood and walked over to a porch post. Leaning against it, he looked his uncle straight in the eye.

"Tal, how come it is that I open this store every morning at 6:00 A.M. for business, and every other store in the entire United States waits until 8:00 or 9:00?"

Tal took a sip and smiled. "You want my answer or Woodrow's?"

"I'm lookin' at you, ain't I?" the boy said boldly.

Tal smiled again. "'Cause Woodrow says and that's good enough for me. Besides I don't stay here anyway. My time's spent out there in God's country. You need to learn, Andrew, that a man just has to believe in things as right and then not worry about them anymore. I believe in Woodrow's ability to declare what time this place opens up. And that's that. It don't make one bit of difference to me what the rest of the country does. They ain't here and I am. You see?"

Andrew shook his head and then walked through the door, pushing his uncle out of the way.

"I'm glad I'm leaving. Yessir, glad as I can be. A man can't never get a straight answer around here. I bet out there a man can get a straight answer, I bet."

Tal followed the boy a few steps and then stopped.

"Hey."

"What?" Andrew said.

"You remember what your old Uncle Tal says. This is straight."
He pointed to the floor. "Out there's the crooked. Here things are
straight."

Andrew balked. "Oh yeah. How would you know? You ain't
never spent any time out there."

Tal smiled. "I've been to Dallas, Texas, and I've been to Toledo,
Ohio, and I've been to a bunch of places my pappy never knew about,
and it didn't take me long to look at the first cottonmouth I ever saw
neither." And he turned to leave.

"Where you going?" Andrew asked.

"Fishing . . . you want to go?"

"No, I better stay. Look, I'm sorry, Tal. I'm just confused."

"You need to go fishing then," Tal answered.

A pickup truck pulled outside, and Sanders McCoy came slinking
in with a battered old Remington Fieldmaster .22.

"Mornin', fellers," he opened. "Woodrow here yet?"

"You know Woodrow don't get here till seven, Sanders," Tal
answered. "What can we do for you?"

"I need to trade guns, that's what. And I can't wait til seven
neither."

Andrew spoke up from behind the display case. "Woodrow does
all the gun tradin'. You know that, Mr. McCoy."

"Yeah, well, the door's open and you're in business to trade guns
and I demand that we trade guns."

Stumpy Dawes entered the room from the adjoining garage where
he did the fish buying. He was built like a vertical bail of hay and a
big one at that.

"Unless you've got a gun in your pocket a lot bigger than that
Remington, you best not demand nothing."

There was a silence in the gun shop as Stumpy's words sunk in.
Tal was still smiling, as Andrew looked nervously from one man to
the other.

"Trade with the man," came the words from the doorway, and
they all turned to see Woodrow Dawes standing there.

Andrew swallowed hard. He looked across the room to his uncle, who was stationary in the door, watching and offering nothing to indicate he had any plans to move.

Sanders McCoy was also watching Woodrow. He nervously laughed, lowering the rifle to his side in a half-hearted attempt to hide it.

"You're here awful early, Woodrow," he offered.

"My store . . . reckon I can show up just whenever the mood strikes me, McCoy. I've got good help, you see. Makes things easier when you trust your help. Now, take Andrew there. Normally, I do all the gun tradin' 'cause it can get kinda tricky, but ol' Andrew's pretty tough, so I'm gonna let him trade with you, and whatever he allows is fair, I'll stick with. Even when you wouldn't take the deal I offered you yesterday. So it's obvious to me that you wanted to trade with the boy, instead of me, so, trade with him."

Now gun trades in Town Creek were the subjects of much debate and personal pride. The rule was that any trade that lasted over five minutes was open to public scrutiny. In other words, if it took a man over five minutes to trade, negotiations must be vocalized so all observers could hear and offer their criticisms or nods of approval. On occasions, a trade might last the better part of the afternoon. The all-time record, at least in this century, was held by the local wildlife officer, who, after stopping by the store to eat lunch, got involved with Woodrow over a Browning shotgun, and had to call the central office to request official leave to complete the trade. His supervisor, a Browning man himself, understood such fits of passion, therefore, approving the officer's request for time off. August was a good time of year to trade guns anyway, with the absence of peak hunting and fishing activities. The trade lasted just over eight hours, plumb through the supper hour, and the general feeling was that both parties came out respectable. It turned into a right sociable event with Stumpy firing up the fish cooker and onlookers eating while the trading and arguing continued. The observing crowd grew to about forty, as news of a good gun trade spreads pretty fast in Town Creek.

As Woodrow stood at the door, contemplating his next move, he sensed that his presence was making the boy nervous, so he walked deliberately through the gun room to the back office and out a side door into another workroom. Stumpy and Tal followed, leaving the younger Dawes to trade guns with McCoy. The three brothers sat at a table cluttered with outdoor magazines, old fishing lures and one turkey box call. Woodrow sipped his coffee and quickly felt the stares from the other men.

"Well," he asked. "What's wrong with you two?"

Stumpy raised his eyebrows before speaking. "I dunno, Brother . . . seems to me you're getting a bit . . . uh . . . what's the word?"

"Mellow," Tal smiled. "How 'bout mellow?"

"Maybe," the shorter brother replied. "Mellow kind of reminds me of Luther's corn whiskey though."

Woodrow picked up the box call and made a perfect purr and cluck, before gently returning it to the table.

"The trouble with you boys is you don't recognize restraint. It comes with maturity and proper amounts of study. But you wouldn't understand 'cause everything's so plain to you . . . so black and white."

"I'll say this," taunted Stumpy. "Sanders McCoy came early to trade when he thought you wouldn't be here, and that is pretty plain to this ol' country boy. Don't take no Philadelphia lawyer to figure that one out, brother of mine, and you let him get away with it. Dang, he'll probably have poor Andrew so bumfuzzled that the kid'll give him the gun he wants and feel good about it."

"He's right, Woodrow," agreed Tal. "You should have tossed ol' McCoy out on his ear and been done with it. Why I remember when you would've. . . ."

"That's what I mean," argued Woodrow. "Black or white; whup him or love him. I've got crazy people on my side."

"Oh, yeah," said Stumpy. "You callin' me crazy?"

"As a certified betsy bug," finished the older brother. "The boy's gonna be leavin' us soon . . . out on his own in the world of higher education—the only Dawes to ever get a college education I might add—and you want me to keep on treatin' him like a kid. He's all grown up, boys, in case you hadn't noticed."

"Dang it, Woodrow. We know that, you old goat. You're the one that's got the boy confused. He's been mopin' around here for a month wanting to talk, and you won't engage him straight up about the mysteries of the world. He's a searching for answers and you're giving him parables."

Tal stood up from the table. "Reckon a man needs to find his own answers, so I got no truck with Woodrow's story tellin', but I'd a still tossed old McCoy out on his ear. I've got no time for weasels . . . and I'll not tolerate one in my henhouse." And the younger brother was gone, leaving Stumpy and Woodrow alone at the table.

Andrew appeared at the door. He crossed behind the brothers and poured his own coffee.

"You ain't through yet, are you?" Stumpy asked.

"Yessir," said the boy. "I told him that he had five minutes to trade with me 'cause I wasn't going into public negotiations. I told him that I was a bit scared about that and whatever we decided he was to never tell Woodrow what we settled on, 'cause I didn't want to be riled about gettin' beat."

"He bought that?" Woodrow asked.

"Like a duck on a June bug," said the boy. "I got $190 and his old Remington against the Ruger he was wanting, and then I sold his Remington to Mr. Winslow for a hundred over the phone. We made money on both deals."

Stumpy's mouth dropped open and Woodrow beamed. "See there, Stump!" prided the older brother. "All grown up."

"I don't know," said Andrew. "I figure you had him spooked about coming in early. He was probably feeling guilty."

"The last time he felt guilty about anything, he was fighting the Japs over Pearl Harbor, back in the forties," replied Stumpy.

"Well, I've got work to do. You did well, boy. Hold down the fort while I'm gone. I'll be back this afternoon." And Woodrow left. They could hear his footsteps on the wooden floor heading north.

There was silence in the room after Woodrow's footsteps faded. An endangered breeze moved the papers on the table and then was gone, letting the heat of the morning build in the room. Andrew looked toward the open window that provided the refreshing breeze and thought he could detect a hint of honeysuckle in the air.

"Most kids I know are really looking forward to leavin' come September," he offered. "I guess I should be, too. But doggone, Uncle Stump . . . I'm gonna miss this place. Is that wrong . . . I mean . . . should I hate leavin'?"

Stumpy Dawes absolutely hated serious questions from the kid, and that's why he was so upset at Woodrow for not addressing these points of child raising. He squirmed in his chair and looked up at Andrew.

"I ain't no good at such questions, Andrew. I mean, I'll just come out and tell you that I'd whup a whole colony of hooligans if I thought they were riling you. I'd walk from here to Nashville with a broken leg just if you ask for a favor, but I cannot engage in such serious questions. I'm affeared that I'll answer wrong and mislead you. And that is something that would pain me greatly, 'cause . . . ," Stumpy got up and walked toward the door.

" . . . 'cause I love you like you was my own boy, Andrew. Dang it, we all do and we're gonna miss you more than you miss being gone."

Andrew watched his Uncle Stumpy leave the room and thought he had never known the man to look so uncomfortable. There was a lump in his throat that just wouldn't go away, and for the first time he strongly considered not going at all.

It was mid-afternoon when Andrew heard the commotion outside the store. Billy Jessup discontinued his debate about how President Bush had betrayed all gun owners with his stand on assault rifles and moved to the window.

"Why it's Woodrow, and he's got the Widow Brubaker with him. Hot dog, boys! It's to be something fine. Whenever Woodrow and the Widow get together, there's fun for sure."

The entire gathering in the store moved quickly to the porch as Woodrow was helping the Widow up the steps. There were perhaps forty or fifty people in procession, following the leaders. The Widow Brubaker breathed hard at the walk up the three steps to the porch. She was dressed in her Sunday attire, which signaled a speech of substance was coming. She collapsed in a rocker, and Andrew noticed a line of sweat beads across her upper lip. The people in the street paused below, forming a congregation of onlookers, all waiting for Woodrow to begin.

Woodrow smiled at the people and then took control, like a preacher in the pulpit.

"It sure doesn't take long to form a crowd in this town," he stated. "But as long as you all are here, I'd like to take this opportunity to announce a special event in the history of Town Creek. Now August is a slow month with the heat and all. Too hot to do much of anything, but I'm here to announce the first annual invitational Town Creek Trophy Frog Hunt. It'll be this Saturday starting at sunrise, which is not your normal time for frog hunting. Most of us grew up huntin' frogs at night, but this is gonna be different. It ain't no frog killing, but a true frog hunt. Now any of us knows how to kill a mess of frogs at night, but this hunt has a special twist. It's a frog hunt where you have to stalk the pond and shoot 'em long range in daylight. Now we all know that the Widow Brubaker is our town's official rulemaker for such events, and I've asked her to study on this project and announce the rules. If you'll give her your attention, she'll give you the guidelines. Her decisions are final, as always. Mrs. Brubaker. . . ."

Andrew watched the crowd. There was a thread of excitement in their eyes. They whispered quietly after Woodrow's opening with nods of approval on the idea. They then turned to the lady on the porch. Andrew followed their stares to the Widow.

She weighed about two hundred pounds and was just five feet tall, but nobody really noticed her obesity anymore. That was just the Widow Brubaker. She was dressed formally, except for the white house slippers, which she always wore . . . always. She rocked in the old chair, using her ironwood cane as a staff, and the audience waited patiently for her to speak. Her voice was strong, but quivered a bit as she spoke.

"Now I know what some of you are thinking. Some of you have already decided to cheat by taking your frogs the night before. Let me emphasize that this activity will not be tolerated. Mr. Harris, the local game warden, will be our official scorer, and he has assured me that there is a test he can run to determine time of death in bullfrogs. If anyone is caught falsifying when their frogs were taken, the penalty will be forfeiture of entrance fees and banishment from any Town Creek function for one month; the forever and ever disqualification from future frog hunts in Town Creek; and all of us will generally think you to be a cheat, which is the worst penalty of all."

The Widow paused, repositioning her lower denture. "The entrance fee will be three dollars per hunter, or one dollar per junior hunter under the age of sixteen. The person who brings in the highest scoring bullfrog will receive all the entrance fees—a sizable prize I might add—of which 10 percent must be contributed to his or her local church in respect to the good Lord who gave us all these wonderful frogs in the first place."

"In order to enter a frog into the official scoring process, the hunter must have taken the legal daily limit of twenty frogs. This ensures that the winner will be a competent hunter of frogs and not just have the knowledge of where a really big one lives. Each hunter can only enter one frog to be scored of the twenty he brings in. All frogs will be donated to the frog leg supper next Saturday night, except the winning frog which will be mounted by Wally Hathcock, our resident taxidermist, who said he'd do it for free. The frog will be displayed at the Town Creek Trading Company for one year and then given to its rightful owner after next year's competition. This contest is only open to the bona fide residents of our town, and the hunt is limited to the river, farm ponds and natural waters of this county that lie within a ten-mile radius of this building right here. Now . . . are there any questions?"

The crowd was studying. The Widow had laid a lot on them in such a short period of time. Finally, Randall Hickerson spoke up from the center of the crowd.

"Mrs. Brubaker, I hate to be belligerent, but doggoned if I know how to measure a danged bullfrog. I can measure a Boone and Crockett deer or a Pope and Young, but I ain't never heard of an official bullfrog score before."

"Well, of course you hadn't," she responded. "It ain't never been done before in the history of the world, so far as we can tell. That's what makes it so fun. Now, the way we figured a man would have to measure a frog in order to capture all the attributes is as follows: measure the total length of your frog and write that down to the closest eighth of an inch. In other words, a ten-incher would be eighty. Now, add to that the total weight of the frog in ounces, 'cause we all know that the heft of a really big frog is impressive. The only other measurement is the distance across his mouth when you open his mouth up all the way—you know from top to bottom. Now, the purpose of this measurement is to take in the frog's croak, for we all can appreciate an impressive croaker, and the only way we could figure how to get the croak was through a mouth measurement."

Well, the last portion of her speech really got them. There was no use in arguing with the Widow. It was obvious that she had figured on everything, down to the frog's croak, and there was no reason in trying to pin her down. The crowd dispersed into several groups, and for the next two hours the talk was centered around honey holes that produced hidden monster frogs. The idea of Town Creek's first annual invitational trophy frog hunt was an instant success. Andrew danged near sold out all his .22 shells and had a run on Tasco scopes. There was real excitement in the air, even from those who didn't frog hunt, in anticipation of the frog leg supper and associated socializing.

It was almost supper time when Andrew and Woodrow decided to close down the store. They walked out onto the porch and took a seat, taking in the coolness of early evening.

"I got to give it to you, Woodrow. That frog hunt idea was the best you've come up with in a time," Andrew said. "The whole town is excited."

"Well, thank you, Andrew. I thought we needed a little boost around here." They rocked for a second as a whip-poor-will started up down on the creek.

"I've got this empty feeling, when I think about leaving here, Woodrow. Is that bad, I mean is it an omen, you reckon?"

Woodrow looked straight ahead and kept on rocking. "Reckon not," he answered. "I figure it's a sign that you might be careful."

The boy stopped and looked at his uncle. "Careful?"

"Yeah . . . that feeling is normal when a man is fixing to change his lifestyle to take in new things . . . things that could make him question his roots, but don't fret. Fact is you may change the way other folks look at things, instead of the opposite."

Andrew looked away. "I doubt that," he said. "What could I teach folks?"

Woodrow smiled. "You just wait. You'll see. This country is crying for folks who haven't lost touch with solid ground. You just remember to keep your head high, 'cause no man respects anyone who doesn't respect himself."

"I don't understand . . . it seems like you want me to leave, and that bothers me. I don't want to leave y'all, and you seem like you want me to go."

"I do, boy. I want you to go. As much as I wish it, I can't keep you from growing up, and the only way for you to understand about the way we raised you is for you to go out and see for yourself if we were true to you or not. I'm not afraid that you'll see straight. When your folks were . . . when they passed away . . . and we took you to raise, I promised myself that I'd do my best to teach you what's important about living. Now, that don't necessarily mean I have to give you an overview of how other people's priorities have got all screwed up. You have to find that out yourself, but these people . . . the people of Town Creek are honorable folks, and it ain't cause we're slow or stupid that we live the way we do. It's a matter of choice. I will tell you this. Life is relatively simple. History tells us that, and happiness can be just as good in Town Creek as in Nashville. A man needs a couple of things to be happy. First he needs a land that is clean, so as to provide a barometer of perfection, and the land is perfect in all her glory and sadness. Next he needs a good job, a job that keeps his mind working and his interest up, 'cause boredom is a powerful killer of the soul. He needs entertainment, and I'm telling you that the greatest entertainment a man can have is proper marriage to a proper woman, but don't go askin' me about women just yet 'cause that gets real complicated real quick. And that's about it, with the exception of good friends to socialize with who share the same feeling about living. Clean woods and waters to do your thinkin' and prayin', a good job that keeps you interested, a good woman for companionship and laughter, and good friends. It don't get any simpler, but I suspect you'll find it to be quite complicated.

"So, you want me to go?" Andrew asked.

"You bet," replied his uncle. "But it's gonna hurt like crazy while you're gone. You just remember that we'll always be here and if you need a place to slow down and collect your thoughts, we'll be here tradin' guns and killing trophy frogs."

Andrew smiled. "Thanks, Uncle Woodrow. That means a lot. I promise I'll do you proud. I promise."

Woodrow got up and slapped the boy on the back. C'mon, let's go get some of your Aunt Clair's supper. I'm starved."

Andrew stood. "I think I'll walk, if you don't care. Tell Aunt Clair I'll be along directly."

The boy watched as the truck pulled away. He took the main road through the middle of town and noticed the sweet smell of the cool dusk. The town was quiet except for a dog barking somewhere off to his left and the whip-poor-will back on the creek. He walked with a new enthusiasm as the talk with Woodrow had given him new confidence. After a quarter of a mile, he noticed Herbie McCintosh sitting on a stump in his front yard. He stopped and Herbie smiled.

"Sure is a nice night, don't you think, Herbie?" Andrew asked.

Herbie shook his head and smiled again.

"Are you drunk, Herbie? Won't you talk to me?"

Herbie raised his eyebrows and shrugged. He then looked around to see if anyone was looking. He definitely did not want to be barred from the frog leg supper on Saturday night.

Andrew whispered. "Just answer me this, Herbie. How come you love this place so much? You never get to talk or anything. You could live other places much easier than here. How come you love it so much?"

Herbie looked around again and spoke without stuttering.

"I guess it's pretty simple, really," he whispered.

Andrew looked amazed. "Why, Herbie, you're not drunk at all! You didn't stutter a lick."

Herbie placed his index finger across his mouth. "Shhh . . . ," he whispered. "Don't anybody to know. I've been quiet so long, I kinda got to where I like it. I really want to keep it that way."

"Why?" Andrew asked.

"I've done a lot of studying over the last six months since I dried out," he began. "Life's pretty simple, really. All a man needs is people who care and land enough to do proper wanderin'. I've got all that right here in Town Creek, but more than anything . . . it's just plain fun livin' here and I'm proud to be a part of it. A man needs some things to be proud of."

Andrew smiled. "I reckon you're right, Herbie. I reckon the mystery is finding out for yourself, so you know, instead of just being told." And Andrew waved goodbye, as he made his way toward Aunt Clair's home-cooked supper. He breathed in a full load of Town Creek air and smiled again, thinking about how much fun it was to just have the chance to stick around, at least 'til September.

The Frog Hunt

Andrew Dawes had decided to completely put away the dilemma of leaving, at least for now. The excitement generated by the anticipation of the trophy frog hunt was just too special to be tainted by thoughts of college.

Town Creek Trading Company had been a beehive of activity since the Widow Brubaker's speech. The idea of daytime bullfrog shooting opened an entirely new arena for township competition. After much deliberation, the general consensus was that any serious competitor must have an accurate twenty-two, capable of consistently placing a well aimed shot into the space of a dime at thirty yards. Approaching a pond closer than thirty yards, unless done with much skill and patience, would result in the entire selection of targets skipping across the water unscathed.

Over the last few days, Woodrow had heard so many tales of hair-splitting accurate rifles that he decided to make his customers demonstrate their skills or shut up. He instructed Stump, who was known throughout the county for his ability to draw, to develop a frog head target, illustrating two protruding eyes above a waterline. Woodrow posted the targets out back at the shooting bench, and quickly there began a whole new competition in Town Creek. Reports from local rifles became commonplace behind the store, and it became very clear, in spite of all the boasts, that rifles capable of trophy frog hunting accuracy were relatively rare in the community. Decorated marksmanship stories slipped to whispers among the patrons, making the conducting of business easier in the store, much to the liking of the Dawes brothers.

It was early in the morning when Andrew Dawes saw Rusty Hill climb the porch steps. The store was already crowded. It smelled of coffee, tobacco, and gun oil. Rusty entered and crossed the room to the counter.

"Mornin' Drew," Rusty began. "Need five boxes of Federal Match."

Andrew smiled. "I heard you might consider taking on clients for the frog hunt."

"Just a rumor," replied the sandy-haired youth. "Had about twenty people ask, but I decided that I have no aspirations to become a bull frog guide."

"What's wrong with a frog guide?" smiled Andrew.

"Since I was twelve, I've been guiding folks for ducks, geese, deer, bass, and turkeys. Frogs are too fun to get serious about. I reckon I'll save my frog hunts for friends."

Andrew grinned. "Shoot, after word gets out about trophy frogs and all the notoriety that goes to the winner, you're liable to see all kinds of new interest in frog hunting."

Rusty threw a ten dollar bill on the counter. "Yeah, they'll probably be sellin' frog calls in the next issue of Cabela's."

". . . and frog scents and pond camo clothes," added Andrew.

". . . and frog decoys and videos on how to be a Town Creek trophy frog championship winner," laughed Rusty.

"So, what about it, friend? You want to go frog hunting? Never can tell. We might get famous and do tennis shoe ads on TV."

"Don't mind if I do. May be our last hurrah before you depart. Tell you what, I'll set up camp in Horseshoe Bottom. It'll be our bullfrog base camp."

From the doorway to his office, Woodrow Dawes watched the two boys laugh, except they weren't boys anymore. He remembered Rusty Hill ten years old and bouncing happily on sacks of corn in the back of his father's truck as it passed the store. He recollected the two youngsters preparing gear for camping trips and their pride in toughness as they matured. He remembered their first interest in girls and how awkward they seemed trying to maintain their toughness around them.

Now, as Woodrow stared, he saw men. Andrew was tall and big-shouldered, but his eyes were sensitive and searching. Rusty was not as tall, but more muscular, sporting arms that could throw hundred pound bales of hay all day and callused hands that could only belong to a farmer. Both were quiet youths, he recalled. The Dawes brothers often questioned, as they watched the two ride off toward some deep woods campsite, if when alone the boys ever talked at all. Now, however, they were all grown up and talking quite well. Woodrow Dawes was suddenly overcome with that thought and the added emptiness of Andrew leaving. He smelled the coffee and the gun oil and the tobacco, and in a split second was completely overwhelmed with the goodness of his life. He turned back into his office where Stump was bent over the adding machine. Stump looked up.

"What's wrong with you, big brother? You look like you been gut shot."

Woodrow frowned. "What do you know about gut shots? You can't even operate a simple adding machine."

"I do so know how to work a danged adding machine," Stump

countered. "The sorry thing don't know its figures, that's all. You ought to send this one back to adding machine school."

Tal Dawes joined his brothers in the office carrying a list of those registered for the hunt.

"If ya'll would quit bickering for just a minute, I need to know when the cut off is for registration. We have a hundred and forty-two so far."

"The Widow said five this afternoon, and I don't figure on going against the Widow," said Woodrow. "Tal, you and Stump close up this afternoon. We need to be making preparations for the cooking. Stump, if everybody limits out, how many frog legs will be cookin'?"

Stump entered the numbers on the adding machine, biting his tongue waiting for the answer.

"Two million, eight hundred and forty thousand," Stump smiled, tearing off the tape. "That sure is a mess of frog legs."

Woodrow smiled at his brother, Tal. "With a financial advisor like Stump, we're bound to be millionaires before we die."

The only problem with the Town Creek Trophy Frog Hunt was its timing. In late summer, most community ponds had been previously harvested, mandating that competing frog hunters search their memories for isolated, hard to reach ponds. Scouting parties had been on reconnaissance missions all week determining exact locations of these forgotten wetlands and what treasures they might hold. Old Hoyt Applegate had bragged on Tuesday that he'd found a frog that was "so big it could eat a Chihuahua dog," and Lizzard Tomlinson let it slip that he had spied a frog on the Pritzer place "that he didn't reckon a .22 would stop." Lizzard vowed he wouldn't get near that backwoods pond with anything less than a .30-caliber carbine, and if he did manage to kill the green monster, without a four-wheeler, he'd probably have to quarter the animal to pack him out. No one could tell a tale better than Lizzard Tomlinson, and when he really got wound up, each eye would take off in a different direction. Licking his lips between words, he gave the impression of an erect Komodo dragon straight from some exotic island. Such reports of trophy frogs, while admittedly stretching the truth, did give rise to a real anticipation of just how big the winning frog might be.

The bullfrog base camp lay at the back of Horseshoe Bottom. Surrounded on three sides by sheer bluff, the campsite was a picturesque as a Colorado postcard. Andrew stopped the truck before entering the bottom and took in the sunset scene.

The camp was like a second home, and Rusty was the ultimate backwoods homemaker. No guide that ever lived, from the darkest bush in Africa to the Canadian Rockies, regardless of age or experience, could rival Rusty Hill in his ability to make tent life comfortable. A guest in a Rusty Hill camp would have all the comforts of home, albeit rustic, which made the comforts even more pleasurable. He worked like a slave with predawn breakfast preparations and was always the last to bed. At an age when most teenagers were lost in high school ceremonies, Rusty Hill had a client listing that would make most adult guides envious. Guiding was all he ever talked about doing, since he was ten. Andrew remembered his friend's relentless pursuit of his trade. There was never football or basketball or baseball or cars or clothes or dances but always trucks and guns and dogs and tents and boats and decoys and books. He digested books about the land and people who shared his passion for the land. Rusty Hill breathed in Hemmingway and exhaled Ruark. He sampled Roosevelt and Isak Dinesen, Thoreau and Leopold. Laughing with Ford, he would switch to the botanical readings of Burroughs and remain equally satisfied. In spite of Rusty's aversion to typical high school ceremonies, the girls adored him.

Andrew drifted through his childhood memories while the truck idled at the fence gap. He could see Rusty standing in the camp across the field. Best friends should not be separated by growing up, Andrew pondered. Easing out on the clutch, the tailgate rattled and the truck moved forward.

After a fine supper of marinated deer steaks, fried potatoes, sautéed onions, and dutch-ovened biscuits, the friends relaxed. The fire popped occasionally, sending a showering of sparks skyward, mixing colorfully with the brilliant stars overhead.

"When do you leave?" asked Rusty.

"Two weeks," Andrew whispered to his coffee cup.

"Just what is it that you're going to study? I mean, what are you going to be when you grow up?" Rusty smiled.

Andrew looked at his friend across the flames. "I have no earthly idea. Four years is a long time. I'm hopin' I'll find my place there."

"Why are you fighting this thing so hard?"

"I am not," Andrew countered.

"You've always been bound for college . . . always made good grades . . . ," Rusty struggled for the correct words. "You've always been a deep thinker, Drew. I figure you're headed for greatness, if you don't worry yourself to death before you get there."

"Greatness?" Andrew asked. "That is worrisome."

An hour later, the two had forsaken the tent for the open sky. They lay in their sleeping bags studying the stars as the coals in the fire glowed with the orange-red, low, fuzzy flames. The moonless sky was magnetically deep, with the stars adding a three-dimensional depth to the blackness, and Andrew sometimes felt as though he could fall up into it. His head would swirl with the feeling, and his stomach would sink with such thoughts of infinity.

"Do you believe in God?" Andrew asked bravely.

Ten feet away, Rusty paused, but the night birds continued their calling.

"Without a doubt. . . . He's here," Rusty whispered. "The Master guide of true wilderness."

"You seem sure of yourself," Andrew tested.

"I'm sure of my ability to read sign," said Rusty. "Godsign is abundant in these parts. I figure a man ain't much of a woodsman if he can't find it."

A barred owl called from the creek, and with it Andrew became intensely aware of the night sounds: crickets, bullfrogs, whip-poor-wills, great-horned owls, mosquitoes, and in the distance a family of coyotes vocalized. It was Andrew's last memory before sunrise.

They had coffee and cold biscuits for breakfast, and before the

sun had stolen the coolness of early morning, the truck was bouncing across the pasture.

"You won't believe what I found yesterday," Rusty said as he
steered around an old groundhog hole.

"What?"

"A pond," he continued. "I heard one frog call from a hollow off
the McCutcheon field, so I beached the boat and went exploring. I
can't figure how the old pond got there. It's real shallow with standing timber. Maybe it's an old sinkhole or something."

"Many frogs in it?"

"Two."

"Two?"

"Just two, but the quality." Rusty smiled. "TV commercial quality."

They left the truck in the McCutcheon field, waded the creek,
and started the quarter mile stalk through open timber. Fifty yards
from the pond they crouched behind a blowdown. Peering between
the exposed roots, they surveyed the pond bank with binoculars.

"You see 'em?" Rusty asked with an excitement Andrew had only
heard in relation to turkeys and trophy smallmouth.

"I think we're undergunned." Andrew laughed. "I have never
seen a frog like that!"

There was one section of the pond bank that was void of vegeta-
tion. It was there, in plain view, that the two frogs sat. Like patient
crocodiles, they protected their space, reminding Andrew of two
sun-bathing sumo wrestlers. They were golden-yellow on the bottom changing colors to a greenish-black on top.

"C'mon, we got to get closer. Stay behind me and let's go real
slow," guided Rusty.

They moved, watching the aged amphibians, fearing that each
crunched leaf would trigger an explosion of the targets across the
water. Thirty yards from the pond, they set up behind a fallen oak.
Side by side, rifle by rifle, staring at the frogs through cross-haired
scopes, Rusty whispered to his friend.

"Take the front frog, Drew. Shoot him in the ear. . . ."

"The other one will jump," replied Andrew.

"Don't worry about the other one. Just shoot your frog in the ear."

Andrew's rifle cracked. Rusty's frog jumped, and the second rifle cracked. In a half a second the drama was over.

"Wait! I think I missed," Andrew yell-whispered.

The first frog still sat there, with no change in its position. Rusty stood up and stretched, extending his cramped muscles. The frog sat there.

"He's finished," the guide said in a normal voice. "Big frogs . . . really big frogs . . . won't move a step when you shoot 'em in the ear. Nice shot, Drew. You always were an excellent shot."

Andrew looked with disbelief at the monster frog on the bank. They moved closer, Andrew expecting with each step to see the animal jump.

"Well, at least we got the one," Andrew conceded. "Nobody could've made the shot you tried."

Rusty waded one step into the water toward a muddied area where the frog had jumped. There was a bloodied string floating from the bottom and an extended webbed foot suspended in the ooze. Rusty grabbed the foot and hefted it above the water.

"Oh ye of little faith," he smiled.

Andrew's eyes grew wide. "What a shot! What a frog! Are you really that good?"

"No, see here. I was aimin' for the ear. I hit him a bit far back. A good shot hits exactly where he aims."

The two friends laughed out loud, and sitting at the edge of the old pond, they examined their frogs. Andrew pulled a tape from his pack. Measuring from the tip of its mouth, the frog was eight and three-quarter inches long, not counting the legs. The other frog was identical.

"That frog wouldn't begin to fit in a quart fruit jar," said Rusty.

Andrew pondered, studying the frogs. "Do you feel strong about entering these frogs?"

"Oh no . . . ," Rusty laughed. "The Dawes in you is fixin' to come out. What've you got planned?"

"Deep thinkers always have a plan," Andrew winked.

Town Creek was a beehive of activity at sundown. Woodrow figured that every resident in the community was present. The Widow Brubaker had the entire procedure organized with her usual effectiveness. There were seven measuring tables manned by the official bullfrog judges, supervised by the local Wildlife Officer. Any frogs that were trophy quality were tagged with the official score and name of the hunter and placed on the exhibition table for viewing. Frogs were everywhere.

The line of participants stretched a hundred yards from the tables, all waiting to have their frogs scored. Lawn chairs and coolers were spread over the Trading Company property like a Fourth of July picnic. Stump Dawes had five propane fish cookers going as well as a whole crew of frog leg skinners at his disposal. The community churches had organized, through their ladies' groups, the dining tables, which were now stacked full of potato salad, slaw, breads, and a vast array of desserts. There were gallons and gallons of iced tea, soft drinks, and lemonade. Laughter erupted from various groups on the grounds at alternating intervals, and a fried frog leg aroma hung over the valley like a fog.

Andrew and Rusty sat on the front porch of the Trading Company taking in the sights and sipping lemonade. Tal Dawes came out of the store, locking the door behind him.

"You two are up to something. What is it?"

"What?" asked Andrew.

"Don't what me, " Tal smiled. "I've been studying you two since you were both suckin' on milk bottles."

"Hey," Rusty whispered. "There they are."

Andrew followed his partner's eyes across the street. The Moffitt twins were struggling toward the activities carrying a wet tote sack and an old Crossman pellet rifle. Their jeans were wet past the knees, and their clothes where mud stained and dirty. With each step, their tennis shoes slopped water. At eleven years old, the red-headed twins were known throughout the community as the most ambitious of the new crop of hunters.

"Were we ever that little?" Rusty asked.

"You were," said Andrew. "You were a runt."

Rusty stood and eased toward the porch edge.

"Hey Jimmy and Timmy! Come here!"

The twins changed course, crossing the street and climbing the steps to the store.

"Y'all do any good?" Rusty pried.

"Yessiree Bob, we finally killed our limit," Jimmy or Timmy replied. No one could ever tell which was which.

"Forty . . . you got forty frogs in there?" Andrew asked.

"Naw," the other twin answered. "Pappa made us earn our own entrance fee, and we couldn't come up with but one, so we asked the Widow, and she said that since we were identical twins and really like one person that we could work together for one entry."

"Well, then it's OK if the Widow says so," added Andrew. "But didn't you hear about her clean rule?"

The twins looked puzzled. "Clean rule?" They both said together.

"Yeah," Rusty agreed. "She said that anybody comin' to supper all muddy and such was disqualified. You boys need to clean up a bit."

Andrew rose and moved toward the store door, unlocking it. Tal left the porch trying to disguise his laughter, shaking his head.

"C'mon with me. I'll let you boys use the sink in here," Andrew offered.

The twins moved toward the door, carrying their sack. "Whoa!" Andrew motioned. "You can't come in here with that old, wet, frog smellin' sack. Rusty'll watch it for you."

The twins studied on that for a second. Jimmy squinted one eye. "We got some bigguns in that sack. I don't want nothin' happenin' to our frogs. You promise you'll take care of 'em?"

Rusty crossed his chest. "On my word of honor, boys. I'll take care of your frogs."

"Well, OK." Jimmy reluctantly handed the sack to Rusty. "We'll be right back."

Andrew winked at Rusty as the two red-headed boys entered the store.

Ten minutes later the twins dragged their sack toward the measuring tables. Andrew and Rusty followed. Last in line, the twins waited patiently. Finally, they handed the sack to Ben Hankins, who untied the string holding the open end together.

"Are they all good and dead?" he asked the boys. "I've had a belly full of dead frogs jumpin' off the table."

Timmy answered. "Yessir, Mr. Hankins. They're all graveyard dead. We double checked, and reshot the ones that dared to move."

From twenty yards away, Andrew and Rusty could tell when the frogs were emptied onto the table. The crowd noise rose as people pushed around the table. Easing close, Andrew saw the twins' faces gazing amazingly toward the pile of frogs. Their eyes were big and white. Their mouths were gaping open. On the table were eighteen medium sized frogs, the largest maybe four inches, and two sumo wrestler monsters, dwarfing the others. Yells erupted from the judging area, and people started slapping the twins on their backs. Lizzard Tomlinson spied the twins' frogs and threw his hat to the ground.

"Sorry on the low-downed luck," he exclaimed. "I've been beat by pygmies."

Ben Hankins tagged the frogs and placed them on the trophy table. There was no need to judge further. The winners were obvious. The Widow Brubaker wobbled over to the table and covered her mouth with her hand, trying to hide her smile.

"My lands," she proclaimed. "Boys, come here."

She immediately led the twins, who were still big-eyed, to the official's table. Picking up the microphone, she began. Woodrow Dawes picked the twins up and stood them on the table for all to see.

"Everybody gather 'round," she announced. "We have just determined the winners of the first Town Creek Trophy Frog Hunt. The Moffitt Twins here have taken perhaps the largest bullfrogs on the planet. We all know these boys and how serious they take their hunting. Well, all their practice and persistence has paid off. Boys, we all congratulate you and would like to know the secret to your success."

She handed the microphone up to the boys who were obviously intimidated by their recent celebrity status.

"Secret?" Timmy asked, jumping back from the mike upon hearing his amplified voice.

The Widow agreed, urging them to talk.

The boys huddled, holding the mike away from their serious whispers. Finally, Jimmy took a deep breath, delivering their response with a loud confidence.

"Prayer."

The crowd cheered and laughed. The boys finally smiled, knowing they had answered honestly. Andrew and Rusty had eased over to the cookers, stealing hushpuppies from Stump's pile of finished products. They looked at each other and smiled. Rusty extended his hand toward Andrew. Andrew took it.

"I don't know what the future holds, Drew, but I want you to know it's been a real pleasure runnin' with you. I'm gonna miss you."

Andrew started to reply, but his throat wouldn't let him. Between the handshake of his best friend and the smell of fried frog legs and sounds of a community of friends and the coolness of the Town Creek night, his throat just would not let him speak. But Rusty knew how Andrew felt. Rusty had always been good at reading sign.

Departure

Andrew Dawes looked down from his sixth floor window of Hess Hall at the solid line of people and cars moving slowly toward Neyland Stadium. Rising like an open-topped mountain against the Knoxville viscera, the stadium spouted powerful eruptions of the Pride of the Southland Marching Band. Below him were thousands of fellow Tennesseans, yet total strangers. He knew not one solitary soul that walked in his vision, and it was the loneliest that Andrew Dawes had ever felt. He had never thought it possible to actually hurt from loneliness, but it was true. It pulled on his stomach like a painful poison, as the Town Creek college student studied the people passing below him. He desperately tried to unravel this strange sign in an unfamiliar country. Andrew would have felt less alone, he reckoned, had he been dropped in the barren tundra of the Alaskan wilderness. What new set of rules was he supposed to follow to feel a part of this proud heritage? Obviously, his Town Creek upbringing had failed miserably in lesson number one, *How to Maintain Your Confidence When Nobody Knows You're Alive.* He looked the opposite direction down Andy Holt Drive, where he detected no end to the parade of UT fans. The entire planet Earth, he figured, was coming to this game.

Remembering the many times he and his friends had gathered around a truck radio while hunting doves or taking a lunch break during bow season, Andrew fought a powerful urge to pack his gear and go home. Just pack and leave. It would be so simple. All the UT fans he knew were in the woods right now listening to John Ward on the Vol Radio Network, and there were more than ninety thousand of them. From Reelfoot Lake to Roane Mountain, from Anderson Tully to Tellico would be hundreds of thousands of woodsmen cheering and cussing today's game plays. Suddenly, Andrew Dawes felt good again. He was not really alone, just misplaced for the next four years. There was a strange power in these thoughts, much like finding a lost trail back to the main road where you had left your truck.

Andrew turned from the window and studied the dorm room, his new home, which was much smaller than his old bedroom. Its confined dimensions contained two built-in desks, two sort-of beds, two mirrors with shelves and two cubbyhole closets. A common walk space separated the two identical halves. He had tried to make his half appear homey and break the monotony of cloned living quarters by the hanging of a magnificent wild turkey fan over his bed with a matching pair of whitetail antlers on either side. Over the mirror was a poster advertising the Town Creek Trophy Frog Hunt with Stump's frog head target positioned along side.

The poster drifted his thoughts back to Town Creek and the day of his departure. Unable to sleep the night before, it had been easy to rise early. Having packed the truck the previous day, there was nothing left to do but leave. The unavoidable confrontation of saying good-bye to Uncle Woodrow and Aunt Claire was temporarily postponed with the idea of a note. Andrew could write a short letter and be gone before they got up, allowing the family to avoid the emotional break, but half way down the steps from his bedroom, he caught the smell of frying bacon rising from the kitchen. Leaning against the wall, he gathered fake strength, before continuing.

"Mornin'," he announced almost too quickly upon entering the kitchen, his presence suddenly stifling the talk between family members. To his surprise, Tal and Stump were seated at the table with Woodrow. Aunt Claire was at the stove turning bacon.

"Have a seat, Andrew. I'll have breakfast ready in a jiffy," smiled Aunt Claire, but Andrew could tell she had been crying.

Andrew poured a cup of coffee and stood at the counter.

"Somebody die or something?" he asked.

"We were just reminiscing," said Woodrow. "When you get older and have children of your own, you'll understand."

There was an uncomfortable pause while everyone listened to the bacon pop and sizzle.

"You sure you don't need us to go with you, Drew?" Tal offered. "You have a lot of gear to unload. Who's gonna help you?"

"I'll get by, Uncle Tal. Appreciate the offer. . . ." Instantly, Andrew knew he could stay no longer. It was crazy to prolong this thing. He swallowed a gulp of coffee and moved to the table extending his hand to his uncles.

"I'm going to push off. Y'all take care and I'll be in touch when I'm settled."

The men rose from the table scooting their chairs loudly against the wooden floor. They each took the boy's hand. Woodrow looked Andrew in the eyes.

"No need to rush off, Andrew."

"Yessir, there is," Andrew replied. "I don't like this much."

Woodrow smiled. "I understand, son. You stand your ground. Remember what we've tried to teach you."

"I will do that, Uncle Woodrow." He moved to Aunt Claire.

"You can't go without your breakfast," she teared.

"Yes ma'am, I can. Not real hungry anyway, but I appreciate your cooking it. You take care of those guys for me." He hugged her, for the first time noticing how small she was.

Andrew Dawes looked back at the house after turning onto the main road from the driveway. They were all on the front porch watching him leave. Aunt Claire was the only one waving.

An eruption of lavanous cheering brought Andrew back from his daydream. He briefly noticed the open math book and the half-finished assignment on his desk before leaving the room. Closing the door behind him produced an echoing "clunk" down the deserted hall. There was no noise, talking, music . . . no sign of life. The building felt totally abandoned, and he wondered if he was the only student inhabiting the entire dorm complex. In the lobby, he found signs of life, sort-of. The same five students were always in the lobby, regardless of the time of day or night. He passed them on the sofas, nodded hello, and exited the building.

The football game was now in progress, he reckoned, and from the quick, distressed roar, he would have bet his truck that an incomplete pass had just occurred. The fan numbers had decreased on the street, and he turned away from the stadium. Walking south, he continued until Andy Holt Drive ended. Andrew crossed the street passing under several urbanized sycamores, crossed railroad tracks and entered a narrow strip of trees. The trees ended at a creek, its water quality questionable. Fifty yards upstream he saw a series of large diameter pipes that crossed the creek.

He climbed higher exploring the base of one pipe, and like a fallen log bridging a creek, there was sign of past crossings. Balancing with arms outstretched, he walked the pipe, as he had crossed logs at home a thousand times before.

Andrew climbed the opposite bank and once again found himself to be on developed property. The grounds were neatly kept, and he immediately noticed the trees were marked with small signs identifying common and scientific names. On a quiet street he continued south observing the vehicles had STAFF parking stickers, reaffirming his suspicion of UT land.

As he approached the next building, a van backed toward a service door, and Andrew watched as a group of young men and women exited the vehicle. The driver, a small man wearing mismatched plaid shorts and shirt, directed the students' work as they unloaded several tubs of what smelled to be fresh fish as detected from Andrew's down-wind position. He also recognized the smell of woodsmoke mixed with the fish, hinting to Andrew of an overnight expedition.

Andrew entered the door behind them, interested in what building could house such activities. He followed their scent trail up two flights of steps and entered a hall. Exploring now, Andrew peeked in each vacant room, finally deciding there was a whole area of the university he had not been privy to, and it pleased him to find new "country" to his liking.

An open door to his left revealed rows of tables with displayed animal skins, each hide numbered with an index card. Also, the walls of the room were adorned with expertly mounted specimens of big game species from Africa, as well as North America. Andrew wandered through the room wondering what class this could be and already wanting to be a part of it.

From the door a man watched as the tall, big shouldered youth moved from table to table. Finally, he asked, "See anything you can identify?"

Andrew jumped, turning to see the form in the door. "Sorry, I was just looking."

"It's OK, that is if you're not in the mammology class that has this practical on Monday."

"No sir . . . you're a teacher? I mean, you don't look like a teacher, no offense."

"It's the light," he smiled. "So, can you identify any of these?"

Andrew moved through the tables as he responded. "Yessir . . . most of them, I think. Let's see, here's a spotted skunk, a cotton rat, mole, shrew, muskrat, possum, flying squirrel, chipmunk, swamp rabbit, beaver, gray squirrel, long-tailed weasel, fox squirrel, cottontail, mink, gray fox, bobcat, red fox, coyote, otter. . . .”

“Where are you from?” the professor asked.

“You've never heard of it, sir. It's real small.”

The teacher moved closer, adding another study skin to a table. “Try me, I'm a small town fan.”

Andrew smiled. “Town Creek, it's just north of. . . .”

“I know where it is. On the banks of the Cumberland River. I was there in seventy-five doing a wood duck float survey. Outstanding country! Traded shotguns in the gun store there.”

“You've been in the Trading Company?”

“Feller, I've traded guns in every gun store in the State, I reckon. It's my passion, trading guns.”

“That's my family's store,” Andrew said. “I hope you didn't get beat too bad.”

“That's the trick in gun trading. Don't ever get beat too bad. A man's gonna get beat, unless the store owner's crazy. You just need to keep your losses to an acceptable minimum.”

Andrew extended his hand. “My name's Andrew Dawes. I really appreciate you letting me look around. It may be hard to believe, but this is the first decent conversation I've had since I got here over ten days ago, which I know doesn't say much for my social skills.”

“Forget the social skills. You know your skins. You want a job, Mr. Dawes?”

“Sir?”

“I need an undergraduate lab assistant. Doesn't pay much.”

“I don't care what it pays. I'll take it.”

“See the secretary in the Wildlife office Monday morning. There'll be some paperwork for you. By the way, you know the scientific names of any of these?”

“No . . . never had much need for scientific names in Town Creek.”

“Well, you are not in Town Creek any more, Mr. Dawes. Learn 'em.”

An hour later, Andrew left the Forestry, Fisheries, and Wildlife building. His new job offer and friendship had heightened his spirits. Not in a pipe walking mood, he chose the much longer route back to the dorm. He was crossing an enormous parking lot, after making about two miles, when he heard the shouting.

At a car, about fifty yards to his right, a girl was backing away from a guy in a fraternity sweat shirt.

"Give me the keys!" he yelled.

"No! You're drunk, Frank! No!" she screamed.

Andrew then noticed another couple at the car. The second girl had her hand over her mouth, obviously upset at the scene. She pulled on her date's arm to stop them, but the watching friend just laughed.

"Give me the key!" the drunk demanded, catching his date by the wrist and slinging her to the ground. Andrew was instinctively closing the distance between them as other spectators were gathering in the area. Andrew watched the drunk, but his view was temporarily blocked when Frank bent over the girl on the ground. He saw the right hand of the drunk extended in the air and heard the girl scream after the swing. Frank rose from his crouched position dangling the keys for his friend to see. His big friend returned the laugh.

Andrew rounded the last car and moved quickly to the crying girl on the ground, who had been joined by her female companion.

"Are you all right?" Andrew asked. The girl had taken the punch in the nose, smudging her make-up with blood and tears.

"What do you think you're doing, cowboy?"

Andrew turned to face the voice behind him when he felt the blow. It hit him high on the right eye, forcing him back against the car. He looked up, seeing the boyfriend in a drunken stupor standing over him.

"Get up, cowboy! I'll give you some more!"

Andrew got up. The sucker punch wasn't much, knocking him off balance more than anything, and Andrew felt stupid for allowing it to happen.

"If that's the best you've got, you're in real trouble, friend," Andrew smiled. "Now, give *me* the keys."

Frank laughed. "Come and get 'em! And, I'm not your friend."

"Where I come from, we don't let drunks talk, much less drive," Andrew said. "And we don't hit ladies, either."

And Andrew hit Frank with a right cross so fast that Frank never saw it coming. The drunk collapsed in a pile at his feet at the same time Andrew felt the body grip from behind him. Frank's partner was attempting a bear hug of sorts and yelling to his friend on the ground.

"Get up, Frank! I got him!"

Andrew suddenly became tickled at the mentality of his attacker, laughing with some difficulty because of the pressure around his chest.

"Frank ain't goin' nowhere," Andrew whispered as he used two hundred pounds of Town Creek muscle to drive the heel of his size eleven Dan Post through a visible Reebok running shoe. There was an agonizing scream behind him, and the chest grip was quickly released. Andrew watched as the big guy hopped on his unbroken foot through the parking lot. Andrew lifted the keys from the limp-handed drunk on the ground and presented them to the girlfriend.

"Here's the keys. It will be awhile before he wakes up. You want me to take you to the doctor?"

The girl attempted to stand, and for the first time Andrew noticed a crowd gathered around them.

"Way to go, buddy!" someone yelled.

"Hell of a punch!" said another.

Andrew was quickly embarrassed. Looking back at the two girls, he smiled.

"Thanks," smiled the second girl. "She's OK, I think. Could you help me get her back to Presidential?"

"Sure," he replied. Andrew put his arm around the injured girl, who had yet to speak, as the three of them headed toward the Presidential dorm complex.

For the first time, Andrew really noticed the second girl. She had long, dark hair and deep blue eyes.

"I'm Andrew."

"I'm Katherine . . . really glad you helped back there. A friend fixed us up with those two clowns for the game, but. . . ."

"I'm glad you're not engaged or something."

She laughed and Andrew noticed her entire face smiled when she laughed. "No, definitely not engaged, or something. So much for my first college date."

"Where are you from?" Andrew asked.

"You've never heard of it, believe me!"

"Try me. I'm a small town fan," he smiled.

"Red Boiling Springs?"

Andrew laughed out loud. "You're right. I've never heard of it."

"Don't laugh . . . it's really a nice place. Don't knock small towns until you've lived in one."

Andrew helped Katherine's friend off the curb. He looked at Katherine as they walked.

"What?" She questioned his look.

"Nothing . . . ," he smiled.

"What? Tell me. . . ."

The Wednesday before Thanksgiving it began to snow. The flakes were big and slow moving, but Andrew's excitement was not diminished because of the weather. The heater in the truck was working well by the time he pulled onto I-40 heading west, and Andrew Dawes was going home for the holiday. Home, where the fireplace radiated security and comfort. Home, where the food was real and its aroma would fill a house. Home, where friends were more like brothers and sisters. Home, where a bed and its blankets could warmly make you glad that it was snowing outside.

"Just where is Town Creek?" Katherine asked.

"That way," Andrew pointed west, "about a hundred and sixty miles passed Red Boiling Springs."

"Do you believe in fate?" she asked.

Andrew looked across the cab at her and smiled, like he was remembering a personal secret. Katherine broke into her own smile, scooting closer and pulling on his arm.

"Well, do you?"

"You mean like some powerful force that determines your path?" he clarified.

"You have to admit," she continued, "it's strange that we're from two really out of the way places and if it hadn't been for those stupid drunks . . . we'd never have met."

Andrew noticed the truck slide a bit on the accumulating snow, and shortly they passed several cars off the road in ditches.

"Put your seat belt on," he instructed, and she obliged, but not allowing the snowy conditions to change the subject.

"Well . . . do you believe in fate?"

Andrew reached down beside his right leg and engaged a small lever.

"I believe," he smiled, "in four-wheel drive. Now, if it was fate that made me choose a four-wheel drive truck so, if need be, I could take you home to meet my family, even if it snowed on a wonderful November night, then I am a firm believer in fate."

Katherine pondered. "It's crazy, but that makes perfect sense to me."

"Good."

"Yes it is. It's very good."

And the kids from Town Creek and Red Boiling Springs continued their trip west, eventually crossing the Caney Fork River five times and talking of fate and winding rivers and what it all meant and where they might go and families and how important it was to have been exactly where they had just come from. It snowed even harder, but they didn't care because they weren't really kids anymore, and Andrew believed in four-wheel drive.

Part III

FIELD NOTES

Oakseeds

December in Tennessee is not normally frigid. My fears of global warming have temporarily vanished, as the back porch thermometer yesterday morning whispered minus ten degrees just before sunrise. The high temperature for the day was four degrees, and the lake my house watches over groaned through-out the day with eerie, echoing ice cries. The wind chill approached minus forty, and I noticed that Tennesseans and their machines do not function particularly well in Arctic temperatures. My Labrador Retriever, on the other hand, gets along quite nicely in the cold. In the yard, he busily chewed one of my best Browning boots without any need of jumper cables to get him started.

Today, the wind has stopped, but the cold lives on. From my tree-stand, I can see the powdering of last night's snow lying on the farm roads below. A white logging trail cuts through the gray-black timber to my right, as if man has teamed up with the Almighty to create a formless piece of scrimshaw. Perhaps from a higher altitude man's scratching into the earth might take an artful form, but if so, I bet it a depressing piece.

In the distance, I hear the first voice of the goose flock. For rural Tennesseans, the effect of passing geese is a wonderfully humbling experience. It lessens everything below and makes us stop. That is good. Like the frigid December temperatures, migrating geese pick us up by our shirt collars and slam us into nature's reality: that we are inescapably a part of non-man, no matter how super-civilized we think we have become. The goose talk, as Aldo Leopold called it, is louder now, and I can see the birds, some two hundred in number, chiseling their way through the sky.

I never hear geese without thinking of Blue-Toothed Bill, the muskrat trapper, who has spent the better part of his life in hip-waders. Bill is a hardened man with massive arms and a left eye tooth that is permanently blue from a long past collision with a Pabst bottle in a bar fight. I once arrested Bill for trapping without permission, a feat which only solidified our friendship. He proclaimed that he disagreed with the law he had broken, and in his mind had done nothing wrong, but understood my job as a wildlife officer. Bill reckoned that one should always try to make something good out of a bad situation, and possibly our friendship was the good that was born through his arrest. I now agree, for Bill's spiritual connection with migrating geese was so touching that it solidified my piecemeal thoughts on the man-nature relationship.

Simply put, Blue-Toothed Bill cannot hear migrating Canada Geese without sobbing. He cannot help it. I have watched him fight it, but the power of the goose talk always wins. It used to embarrass the trapper, but in his maturing years he learned to accept the tears as a spiritual kinship with the land. The first time it happened in my presence, we were standing on a wooden bridge ten miles from the nearest paved road. It was snowing, I remember, and as the geese passed overhead I heard him sobbing.

"What's wrong, Bill?" I asked, but he waved me off, unable to talk. When the goose talk faded, he wiped his eyes.

"It just happens," he whispered. "It just happens."

Bill's dilemma has happened many times in the presence of many different people. I find it refreshing that even for those who do not understand the power of goose talk, no one seems to laugh or even snicker at a man who cries at the sound of migrating birds. Perhaps, however, their reluctance to ridicule has something to do with the fact that his arms are the size of cross ties.

The geese above me are gone now, peculiarly enough, heading north. I wonder what that means. I guess I should know. In contrast to man pilots, I doubt that geese ever doubt their instruments. With these temperatures, I reckon it could be warmer to the north.

Staring down through the arthritic limbs of my red oak, I see a fox squirrel is in search of an acorn in the leaves below. For those who have never tried it, viewing the land from a tree can be quite meaningful. I grew up climbing trees and never really grew out of it. To the contrary, it has become an important part of my life, my time spent in trees. From September through early January, if I needed an alibi for climbing, which I don't, I hunt deer from trees, as do hundreds of thousands of Americans. The meat for my family's freezer is admittedly second in importance to my meditation astraddle an oak limb. The solitude of tree-time soothes me; there is comparatively little gunfire and few arrows thrown from my trees. We eat what I harvest, but my time in the tree is the thing itself, the spiritual nourishment which cannot be provided through the consumption of the deer's red meat. These two nourishments go together, and one is no good without the other, for together they represent the bond between man and the land, and man and the spirit. To kill without the spiritual awareness is wrong, and likewise, to be in spiritual tune without a sense of earth bound tethers is pure hypocrisy. As I said, they go together.

I lost one of my favorite trees to lightning this year. I stood beneath its exploded trunk and mourned its shattered body parts. I found a segment of one limb, worn smooth from the hundreds of hours of my boots on its surface. I looked for my back-rest limb and its trimmed branch that held by pack, but it was lost in the vertical shredding of the lightning's impact. Nearing its war torn body, I looked inside the massive trunk, now split in a twenty foot lesion. Unlike its cousin-mammal relatives, the tree's entrails were clean and sweet smelling, and I could find no repulsive decadence in its demise, other than my inability to replace it. The tree's death bothered me, purely a selfish bothering I admit, for the population of oaks in the stand was quite healthy. As wildlife managers, we are taught quite early to concentrate on populations of life, not individuals. Professionally, I agree with that position, but I was bonded to that individual life form, that good red oak. It supported me as I learned from its position. It elevated me like a great hand so that I could look down on life under me. I looked around for another hand to hold me up so that I might view that same area in the future. I noticed that only from that position could I see all that I needed to see, a hidden honeysuckle thicket to my right, a faint side trail to my left, a portion of the winter wheat field in front. Besides, that tree fit me. It was easy for me to stay there, and I am reluctant to change positions. . . .

. . . but out of necessity this year I chose another tree some fifty yards from the original. I witnessed from my new tree a different angle, the same lessons from below with a different twist, for after I took a chain saw and reduced my old tree to firewood, it left an open space that I could view perfectly from the new location, an open space that before the lightning would have been impossible for me to observe. I pondered these thoughts one cold night while feeding a familiar boot worn piece of oak into the fire.

Tennesseans have a traditional kinship with good oaks. The reduction of native oak stands for merchantable pine forests by the timber companies have brought about a wonderful restoration of land-awareness concentration. The replacement of acorns with pine cones is blasphemous to most locals. Large clear cuts bring wailing and the gnashing of teeth. Does the ownership of land include the moral responsibility of land heritage maintenance? If corporate land holders own title, does it include the right to modify the land's personality?

Yes. The law prohibits not the shift from seasonal color change to evergreen, but there are real world ramifications in the face lifting of mother earth, for even real women who change their hair color experience behavioral modifications. Arguments over hair color continue; however, the only sure thing is the change itself. Our society has mandated the change from oak to pine, with the subtleness of an over buxom cheerleader bouncing by the second string team on the sidelines. The real game ain't on the field, folks. It ground swells in clear view of the stands, but no one seems to catch it, except for the timid water boy who watches everything, but is powerless to enter either game.

Meanwhile, man's lightning storm continues to consume our largest tracts of standing oaks in central Tennessee. I shared lunch on the tailgate of my truck with a local cotton farmer as we overlooked a recent seven hundred acre clear-cut. He carefully placed a sardine on a Saltine and drenched it with Louisiana Hot Sauce.

"Makes me want to puke," he crunched.

"Why's that?" I asked.

"Look at it! Hell, it ought to be against the law. What's an animal supposed to eat out there?"

"Deer will love it for a while, with all the new growth." I doused my own sardine with the red juice.

"Well," he replied. "I don't hear the squirrels cheering real loud over the change."

"I'd rather replace oaks with pines instead of a cotton field," I argued.

He slammed the sardine can down on the tailgate, splattering mustard sauce across my knee.

"And I suppose you don't like them cotton jeans you're wearing?" he said with a quivering upper lip.

"I like my jeans, and I also want to keep wiping my backside with soft tissue paper. It's all of us, Mr. Winslow. It's all of us to blame."

The farmer sighed. "I'm eighth generation Tennessean," he said. "They ain't got no right cutting our trees."

"Our trees . . . ," I pondered out loud. I raised my R.C. in a toasting position. "Well, Luther, let's just go puke and be done with it."

Despite the obvious pressure to change our land for civilized goals, the Tennessee countryside is still a wonderfully beautiful place to pass our lives. The country folk maintain a closeness to the earth in spite of satellite TV. There are farmers and cattlemen and plenty of country stores that sell hot souse sandwiches and pickled pig feet. They keep up with each other's progress and illness. They, for the most part, attend church on Sunday morning. It is a land, however, caught in the middle of a conflict between land based values and the fleeting deception of super-civilization.

Blue-Toothed Bill is the symbol of our unrest. He, like all of us, lives in mortal fear of the geese, and the mystery, in itself, is the prize.

Marriage

It had been bitterly cold when the dog died, perhaps the coldest ever for December. At ten below, it was too cold to dig a proper grave and finish it, offering due respect to a family member, even though he was a dog. Dogs and horses were family members here. Tonight, for example, in the midst of all those people, there was a box in the corner containing the bitch and her pups, direct descendants of the old dog that had died. And as we watched the box, the big man in overalls talked about the old dog and the way his life had ended. I could hear maybe twenty different conversations in the room, as parties are like that, talks and laughs and words and . . . he didn't hear them. I could tell, because he was talking about the old dog, his friend, whose absence was painful. His deep voice quivered and his eyes left mine, searching the ceiling as he tried to control his trembling lips. I've never known a strong man who didn't cry at the death of a good dog, for a good dog is the best of all the good friends, lovers, wives, and family rolled into one bag of hide and hair. The loyalty is the thing. Loyalty is the thing that makes tough men cry. And, although I didn't know it quite yet, loyalty was the theme for the evening.

I had liked his wife the first time I met her, even though she was a bit stand-offish. She was polite, but cool, letting a stranger know quickly that she would protect her husband. I could tell that she loved him a great deal, which made me like him even more. She fit the place, the farm I mean. It was like the farm was woven around them, and they into the land on the hill with the house, and the barn, and the garden, and the dogs. Nothing should interfere with the weaving process, she had subtly showed me. It's not complete. Not yet. We are weaving the farm around us, she smiled. Our strength is in the loom, the farm. I got that the first time I saw her. She confirmed it tonight, and he joined in, the man with the deep voice who mourned the old dog's passing.

They finished the weaving at the fireplace later that night. The renewal of their vows whispered of a mature love. Always. It was so real, in fact, that the wedding ceremony itself tended to wrap the audience into the fiber of their farm, and in so doing, joined all there into their love, by way of the farm, and the food, and the fireplace, and the dogs in the corner.

I'm not sure they knew what they were doing to us, we who were watching. Perhaps, it's not important, but in the joining of two souls, I found it wonderfully divine that they would include the spirit of their love in the ceremony, namely friends who understood, dogs in the corner, dogs on the porch, horses in the barn, and a freshly dug grave containing the essence of their loyalty to each other. For in the old dog's absence, the hurt was replaced by a ceremony . . . a gravemaker of substance.

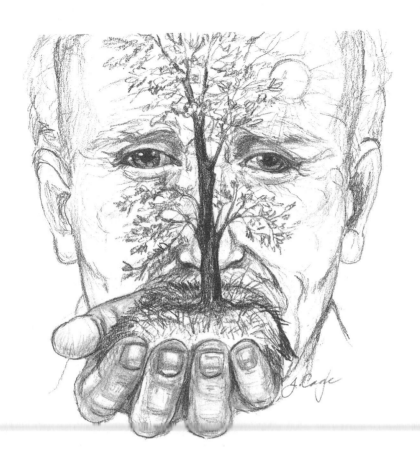

The Last Page

The Old Man died five years ago. His absence has been difficult, not because I have problems with death, but more simply, I just miss him. I miss more than anything his eyes, the way he saw things. His vision allowed him to quickly unravel disguised truths and lay them out in a manner that made a mockery out of complication.

I also miss his love affair with the land. It was a beautiful, romantic marriage of his eyes, his heart, and his boots upon Tennessee ground. His departure from this world left me with an apathetic blandness. He would have been disappointed in me, I think, for allowing it to happen. The colors of fall were not as magical, the calls of geese turned my head slower, the smell of woodsmoke around a campfire was not breathed in as deeply. His death was a struggle for me.

I never had intentions of returning to his old home place. The thought of another occupying his rooms, or the empty house in a state of disrepair would have done nothing to lift my spirits. Places that were once alive with the presence of their owners become terribly depressing when abandoned.

On a turkey hunt in Stewart County, I was told about the way he had wanted it to continue. Again, even after his death, he had surprised us. In his will, he had instructed the family to allow his friends the opportunity to keep the place alive. He wanted John Russell to farm the land, maintaining the Old Man's ideas of respect for the farm's natural value, which included all species of life that currently resided there. He set aside a fund for youngsters in the community who might be interested in tending the yard. The local garden club adopted his flowers as a perpetual project. The house was to be used by his friends for their pleasure, whether it be hunting or fishing or reading or thinking or remembering. When the house falls, he wrote, so will my friends be gone. Then, he continued, so be it.

I pulled into the long driveway and stopped. The house had been recently painted. The yard was deep green, and the smell of freshly cut grass invaded my truck. The autumn olive hedge was larger than I remembered, and the mockingbirds yelled from the trees. Day lilies bordered the barn, and the azaleas grew fat and healthy against the house. I heard young bluebirds crying for food in a box on the fence, and as I continued toward the house, gray squirrels ran for cover in the large oaks.

The key was under the porch, just as Henry had said it would be. The long front porch housed ferns growing from four hanging pots, and three hummingbird feeders were spaced between them. The porch swing was dustless. Its chains were rust-free.

I opened the front door and let the sunlight from the yard invade the house. His hunting coats still hung on the rack by the door, and there was a worn, but polished, pair of Browning Featherweights underneath them. I noticed beggar lice still in the boot strings. Nothing had changed. Nothing.

Moving from room to room, the memories returned. The den contained his guns and books. Guns and books had always been around him. I opened the cabinet and inspected his double-barreled Ithaca, careful to touch only the wood. There was a fresh coat of oil on the bluing. Breaking it down, I checked the bores. They were clean and shiny, just as he would have left them. The smell from the gun cabinet spilled out into the room. It was a faint scent of old gunsmoke, Hoppes #9, linseed-oiled wood, and a mysterious mixture of old quail feathers, deer hides and wet Labs.

I studied his books, arranged neatly in the big shelves by his reading chair. There was Hemingway, Ruark, Faulkner, Twain, Dinesen, Maclean, Thoreau, Burroughs, Ford, Leopold, Buckingham, London and some I did not know. He had used whatever was handy to mark pages, and it was apparent that he had read many of them in the woods, for dried flowers or honeysuckle vines were visible from the pressed pages as if the plants had sprouted, bloomed and died within the books themselves.

I moved into the kitchen with its open windows and sunlight. In the center of the table were salt and pepper shakers made from hollowed out deer antlers and assorted bottles of peppered vinegar, Tabasco, and Louisiana Hot Sauce. I opened the back door allowing the shaded yard breeze to enter the room, filling the kitchen with the smell of honeysuckle and mint. Touching the screened door, I opened it slightly, hearing the squeaking spring. I had heard that spring a hundred times before as he emerged from the house, gun in hand, ready to go.

The man turned the corner of the house and stopped when seeing me at the door. A stranger to me, I did not recognize his face as a friend of the Old Man. He sported a full beard and long hair.

"Hello," I said through the screen.

"Are you supposed to be here?" he asked.

I stepped out onto the porch. The spring groaned behind me. "Yes, I've made arrangements for the weekend."

"You're a friend of Sam Kenton?"

"Yes, I was."

"What was his wife's name?" he asked without smiling.

I smiled. "I called her Miss Sarah."

"Mr. Sam, he had a black dog die a few years before he passed away. They were real close. Would you be knowing the dog's name?"

"He called him 'Old Black Dog' mostly. The papers said Dusky, though," I remembered.

The bearded man came forward and extended his greasy hand. I shook it.

"I was just passing by and saw your truck. No offense, Mister. We just kind of keep an eye on the place for him, you understand?"

"I appreciate it," I said. "By the way, you wouldn't happen to know what kind of shotgun usually went along with the Black Dog, would you?

He smiled this time, removing his grease-stained cap and repositioning it exactly in the same place on his head.

"It was a Ithaca double gun, bored full and full. Kinda partial to number fours."

"Yes, it was," I said.

"You have a good day," he smiled. "I'll see you around sometime, maybe." He turned to walk away, and I noticed a Colt .45 auto stuck behind his belt. He turned back, as if forgetting something.

"Did you ever hunt with Mr. Sam down on the Wilson Place?"

I thought. "No, I can't say that I have."

We stared at each other for a second. "Well, you should have. We had some fine times down there," he finished.

"I know what you mean," I said. He turned the corner and was gone.

I found the journal by accident. I had just made some iced tea and was headed to the front porch to sit while the sun went down. I stopped for a book and when pulling *A Sand County Almanac* from the shelf, the journal fell to the floor. I immediately recognized his handwriting on the paper. Dated upon entry, there were hundreds of pages. I closed it and continued to the porch. Finding a comfortable chair, I opened the book to the last page. His hand was shaky. It was dated February 12, 1987, the day before his death. I closed the book again.

A whip-poor-will started up on the road, and a barred owl answered behind the house. There was no wind, and the leaves hung heavy from their limbs. I looked down at the wooden porch floor. There were scratch marks in the paint made by some black dog of the past. I had seen the dog there at his knee while he talked to it in a deep voice with his wrinkled hand rubbing gently behind its ear. I opened the book to the last page. His words talked to me.

> *The last page of this book ought to be the best. I've been writing in it for so many years, strictly for myself, and I've found a real need to put things down. Everybody ought to keep one of these books. Brings me all sorts of fun to look back in the early years and see how stupid I was, but danged if I didn't have the energy. I've had a lot of blessings in my life.*
>
> *And I've done my dead level best to figure things out. Sarah always said I thought too much. Well, a man is what he thinks. That's a fact. A man is a direct product of his thoughts. Nothing more. Nothing less than the fruits of his thoughts. And this book is a collection of my thoughts and this being the last page, it becomes the last of me. I would hope I wouldn't lie to myself.*
>
> *The land is the center of it all. The land. My relationship with the land has been the secret to my thoughts. It took me a while to realize it, cause I took it for granted, like everybody else. The land is our mother and our enemy, our father and our spiritual guide. It was here first, before us. It will be here after us. It is the only real clue to our existence.*
>
> *The land provides us our most important ingredient for happiness . . . she gives us our struggles. I have come to understand that the greatest friends have been my personal struggles. Ain't that a slap in the face.*

From the very beginning, we have fought the land for our survival. It has not changed now, but there are a great number of people so far removed from the land that they sadly don't know it. She still gives and takes, providing each of us our own set of life's struggles. How we handle them reflects our thoughts, our faith that there is a purpose in all this.

The purpose is grand. I have clues to its grandness. Sunrise. Sunset. The sweetness of spring. The love of my wife. The laughter of my children. The hand of a friend. The voice of my mother. The strength of my father. Wobbly kneed fawns and nursing puppies. It is beyond me the grandness of my life, the things I have seen, the feelings in my heart. It is beyond me, but the land is the center of it all.

No, you say. It is the human spirit that is the center. The spirit is the purpose of it all, not the center. Without the land, the spirit would have not been tested. It would be like some great athlete with no race to run, a painter with no colors, a musician with no sound. The land has been my race, my colors, my strings.

It is all so perfect. In understanding the perfection of it comes a greater understanding of its origin. Perfection is not random. It is divine.

And so, I face my final struggle. Knowing that it is a friend, borne of a perfect land, I will embrace it. I will leave with a smile on my face and a black dog at my side. My only concern is that the dog will not understand my absence. I pray that she will not think I have abandoned her.

I closed the book. I listened to the land, and it spoke to me with the dusk sounds of late summer in Tennessee. Every sound seemed much more important to me, not incidental, but purposeful. And the Old Man's voice was in those sounds, adding a color, a bit of music to the night.

Oakseeds was designed and composed by Kay Jursik at The University of Tennessee Press on the Apple MacIntosh using Microsoft Word ® and Aldus PageMaker ®. Linotronic camera pages were generated by Typecase, Inc. The book is set in Galliard and is printed on 60# Thor White recycled paper. Manufactured in the United States of America by Braun-Brumfield, Inc.

DOES IT ALWAYS RAIN IN THE RAIN FOREST?

Questions and Answers About Tropical Rain Forests

BY MELVIN AND GILDA BERGER
ILLUSTRATED BY MICHAEL ROTHMAN

SCHOLASTIC NONFICTION

CONTENTS

KEY TO ABBREVIATIONS
cm = centimeter/centimetre
ha = hectare
kg = kilogram
km = kilometer/kilometre
km² = square kilometer/kilometre
kph = kilometers/kilometres per hour
l = liter/litre
m = meter/metre
°C = degrees Celsius

Text copyright © 2001 by Melvin and Gilda Berger
Illustrations copyright © 2001 by Michael Rothman
All rights reserved. Published by Scholastic Inc.
SCHOLASTIC and associated logos are trademarks and/or registered trademarks of
Scholastic Inc.

No part of this publication may be reproduced, or stored in a retrieval system, or
transmitted in any form or by any means, electronic, mechanical, photocopying,
recording, or otherwise, without written permission of the publisher. For information
regarding permission, write to Scholastic Inc., Attention: Permissions Department,
555 Broadway, New York, NY 10012.

Library of Congress Cataloging-in-Publication Data

Berger, Melvin.
   Does it always rain in the rain forest? : questions and answers about tropical rain
forests / by Melvin and Gilda Berger; illustrated by Michael Rothman.
      p. cm. – (Scholastic question & answer series)
   1. Rain forests – Juvenile literature. [1. Rain forests—Miscellanea. 2. Questions and
answers.] I. Berger, Gilda. II. Rothman, Michael, ill. III. Title.

QH86.B397 2001   578.734—dc21   00-059460

ISBN 0-439-19383-4

Book design by David Saylor and Nancy Sabato

10 9 8 7   08 09 10

Printed in the U.S.A.   08
First trade printing, April 2002

Expert reader: Mark Halvorsen, Tropics Zone Keeper
Central Park Wildlife Center
New York, NY

The bird on the cover is a toucan. An anteater is on the title page.
The bird on page 3 is a fork-tailed wood nymph hummingbird.

For Brian Erly, a budding scientist
— M. AND G. BERGER

To my wife, Dorothy, and my daughter, Nyanza
— M. ROTHMAN